Hexes & Hot Flashes

THE ORACLE OF WYNTER

USA TODAY BESTSELLING AUTHOR

LISA MANIFOLD

HEXES & HOT FLASHES

THE ORACLE OF WYNTER BOOK ONE

LISA MANIFOLD

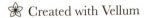

To my sons.

You are my favorite creations.

CHAPTER ONE

I rubbed the bridge of my nose, trying to wish away the headache that was steadily growing. I could feel it—it had been there all day. I knew what was causing it. I'd slept badly, tossing and turning, throwing the blankets off and then pulling them on as I went through hot flash after hot flash last night.

Not to mention, it was my birthday. Today, I was forty-five. Too young for hot flashes, but my body didn't seem to care. I'd already heard from the kids. Theo, Rachel, and Kris had all called me, with varying takes on what I needed to be doing. Later today, I'd be at a spa, being pampered within an inch of my life. It was perfect.

Except for one thing.

My husband wasn't here.

Tears filled my eyes for the hundredth time in less than twelve hours. Derek wasn't here, and he would never be here again. He'd died, almost six months ago, while testing a new chopper. Derek—we—owned a helicopter tour company that operated in the Grand Canyon. He was gone half the year, usually, sometimes more. I hadn't liked it, but I lived on Martha's Vineyard, in my parents' old house, and I didn't want to move to Arizona for six months of the year. Mom had given it to us after we got married—she was worried since I dropped out of college to marry Derek, and I was only twenty. I loved the town of Oak Bluffs, somewhat secluded out on Martha's Vineyard, and the schools, and at the time I had a lot of family around. That had come in handy when I was raising the kids.

Now it was just me. My parents were gone, my aunts were all gone, my childhood friends had moved away, and now my husband was gone.

He was never coming back.

I was alone.

I dashed at the tears as the doorbell rang. "Coming," I croaked, and I hurried to the foyer. A delivery man stood behind a large display of flowers—roses, of all the cream and pink and peach shades.

My favorites.

"Wynter Chastain?" the man asked.

"That's me," I replied.

"Happy birthday," he said, handing over the huge vase. Then he bounded down the stairs and was gone.

I closed the door carefully, not wanting to drop this huge thing. The kids must have sent this. I maneuvered it to the kitchen, seeing why the delivery man was so pleased to be rid of it. It was heavy as hell. While searching among the blooms, I found myself surrounded by the wonderful, heady scent of the roses. Finally, I found the card, and sat down at the island. My name and address were on the front.

Once I got it out of the envelope, I stared at the little card in my hand, my mouth falling open.

It was Derek's handwriting.

Happy birthday, babe! Here's to another great one! Let's have dinner tonight, and dance in the moonlight!

Love from the luckiest guy on the planet,

Derek

I put my head down on the island and sobbed.

I might have slept there, clutching that stupid card in my hand, but the phone rang. Even though I ignored it, the person on the other end kept calling.

"Fine," I groaned, and I slid off the barstool to pick up the phone. It was old-fashioned, but Derek always insisted on a home phone, not trusting cell service when he was out in a place with less than reliable phone service.

"Hello," I said.

"Wynter! Thank god. I've been trying to reach you. Are you all right?" It was Cody Larson, one of Derek's friends from college, and our insurance agent. I'd sent him an email last week wanting to discuss the policy that Derek had taken out ten years ago after a scare at work. He'd upped the payout, telling me that he wanted to make sure the kids and I were taken care of. I'd gotten the death certificate from the state, and I'd contacted Cody to see what the next steps were on his end.

"I'm fine, Cody, thank you. I'm sorry I didn't answer before," I said.

"I got your email, and I've been working on the paperwork, but I've hit…" Cody's voice faltered. "I've hit a bit of a snag. Can I come by and see you?"

"Oh, well, I was planning on—" I didn't get to finish. Last week, knowing it was my first birthday alone, Shelly, my best friend, older than me by ten years, and my friend for over twenty, booked us an appointment for a massage, a fascial, and a pedicure. I'd balked, but she told me that I should agree since I wasn't being given a choice.

I'd agreed immediately. I rarely won when I went up against Shelly.

"This can't wait, Wynter," Cody said.

Something in his voice struck a note of panic in me. It was brief, flaring like a flash of sunlight that blinded when you were in the car on a busy highway, but it was there. "Sure," I said. "Come on over."

"Thanks, Wynter. I'm leaving the office now." He hung up.

I stood for a moment looking at the handset. Something wasn't right. Rather than dwell on what it might be, I went and washed my face and tidied my hair so I didn't look like I'd been collapsed on my kitchen island crying my eyes out. Then I started a pot of coffee, and got the coffee things ready. When Cody rang the doorbell, I was calm, ready for whatever step that would need to be managed. Nothing had been easy since Derek died. Everything took longer, took more effort. I sighed. No reason why this should be any different.

"How are you?" Cody said as he came in, his hands brushing against his pants.

"I'm as good as I can be," I said. I wasn't going to tell him about my birthday, or the flowers from Derek. "Thanks for coming over."

"I wanted to talk to you in person," Cody said. He noticed the flowers as we walked into the kitchen. "Wow. Those are beautiful."

"Thank you. Derek had them sent. It's my birthday today." I tried to keep my tone matter of fact.

"What?" Cody said, his voice dropping to a whisper. "Today's your… birthday?"

I nodded.

He didn't say anything but stared at the flowers as though they were condemning him to execution.

"Well, have a seat, if you'd like," I said, wanting to move past his obvious shock and discomfort. This didn't bode well, but I might as well take the bull by the horns. "Would you like some coffee?"

"Sure," he said, his shoulders hunching up. "Um, yeah. That would be great." He sat down quickly at one of the chairs in front of the kitchen island.

I got cups from the cupboard, and put together the coffee.

Strangely, Cody didn't try and make small talk. Although it wasn't that strange. No one knew what to say to me anymore. I saw it with everyone, even with people who'd known me for years. They just didn't know how to talk to the widow. It had been difficult at first, but I was used to it now. I didn't bother to try and fill the silence. That made things even worse.

I handed over a cup of coffee to Cody and gave him a spoon. I leaned against the counter, sipping from my own cup and waited.

"So, well…" Cody cleared his throat, and set the cup down with a firmer than normal hand after taking a large drink. "I know that you set up the policy with a large payout to make sure you were covered in case anything happened."

"Exactly," I said. "Do you need a copy of the death certificate?"

"No," his first two fingers tapped on the island counter. "We have ample proof of Derek's… death." He looked down, refusing to meet my eyes.

I felt my face crinkle into a frown of concern. Something was off. Wrong. Maybe even really wrong. "Cody, what is it?"

He finally looked up as he sighed deeply. "I know that you and Derek took out a big policy for not only you and the kids, but the business concerns, and anything else that might come up as well. And we're ready to pay out the policy. There's just one more thing we need."

"What's that?" I asked.

"The beneficiaries have to sign off on the split."

I blinked, not sure I'd heard him correctly. Then I took a breath. "I'm sorry, can you repeat that? What do you mean, beneficiaries? I'm the only beneficiary on the policy."

Cody's shoulders hunched again, making him look older than he was. "No, you're not."

"What?" I wasn't sure I heard him right.

"A little over a year ago, when Kris finished college, he came in to change the beneficiaries."

"To whom? The kids?" I shrugged. "That's all right, then." Kris was the youngest, and getting them through school had been a chief concern. With three kids born one right after another, the last couple of years had been tough.

"No," Cody said. "Not your kids."

Something in the way he said 'your kids' made me look harder at him. "Okay, Cody, you're not making sense, and frankly, you're scaring me. So just tell me whatever it is, and we'll sign and be done with it."

"You have to sign off on the split of the payout," Cody said.

"With who?"

"With Natalie Chastain," Cody replied. "His... other wife." He looked away, the coward.

My mind whirled. I knew that Cody was saying something, but I couldn't hear him over the roar in my head. His other wife? What in the utter hell? We'd been married for twenty-five years. *I* was Mrs. Derek Chastain! There was no other Mrs. Chastain. Period. The roar grew and I turned away from where Cody sat at the island, putting my hands over my face. I stumbled, catching myself against the stove, and stood there, letting the roaring race through my head.

His other wife.

His other wife.

When the roaring subsided, I turned to face Cody again. "His other wife?"

He nodded, and I couldn't miss the relief on his face that I was still standing and sounding reasonable. "Yes. Her name is—"

"I know her name," I said sharply. "You said it before."

"She and the kids—"

"The *kids?*" I asked. "My kids are 'the kids'. No one else!"

"Wynter, regardless of the status of the marriage, he split the policy between you and Natalie, because the—her—kids are still little. Your kids are grown."

"What is the split?" I asked.

"Twenty percent to you, the rest to her."

"What?" I whispered. We'd taken out this policy, paying a hefty sum for it, so that I'd have an ample amount in retirement, and we'd be able to help the kids as they moved into adulthood. They didn't have much in the way of student loans, but they were all still renting homes. None of them were ready to buy a home yet. I'd been clear with Derek that I wanted to help them with when they were. We'd talked about it, planned for it, and paid through the nose for this damn policy. And now he wanted our work, our planning, our bearing the cost, with three kids in college at the same time, I might add, to go to someone else?

"No," I said. "That was paid for out of our funds, and it was designed for this family. Not Natalie Whoever."

"Derek changed the policy himself," Cody said quietly. "I'm sorry, Wynter. He was very clear. You have to sign off on it, or you won't be able to collect anything."

"What?" I whispered again. "I don't have a choice?"

"I'm sorry. No." Cody reached down into his backpack and pulled out a folder. He shuffled some papers, and then pushed one across the island to me. "You just need to sign here."

I pulled the paper to me slowly, not wanting to read it. It would make things real. When I'd gotten the death certificate, I'd put it in the junk drawer for four days, unable to look at it right away. Because once I did, it would be real. Derek would be gone. The same was true now. Once I read this piece of paper, whatever it was, there would be no going back. Natalie, her kids, all of it—it would be real.

I looked down, trying to take my time, to focus. This was important even as it felt my heart was being split as it was wrenched from within me. I had to protect myself, even as all I wanted to do was rage and cry and run over Derek with my car for putting me in this situation.

The document was simple. It listed Wynter and Natalie Chastain as the beneficiaries of Derek Chastain's life insurance. It showed the origination date, and then, just as Cody said, showed that last year, Derek had changed it, along with the percentages he wanted to go to each of us. No reason why, no notations.

Then down at the bottom, it had a place for both of the beneficiaries to sign. My eyes widened as I saw a neat, looping signature below where I was supposed to sign.

Natalie Chastain.

His other wife.

"She's already signed this?"

"She sent in the death certificate before you did," Cody said, having the grace to look abashed.

"I'm sure," I said. "If I was getting eighty percent of something I didn't pay for, I would as well." This damn policy had been a sacrifice, even with the success of the business. And now, someone else would benefit from our—my—sacrifice. It burned. A lot. A raging hot fire that sat down deep within me.

"Wynter—" he began.

I held up a hand. "There's no choice in this?"

"None. I'm—"

"Don't say you're sorry again, please. I need a pen." I held out my hand. I was pleased that my voice didn't tremble, that my words were steady even as I was shaking with anger.

Cody produced one with what seemed like great haste. I scrawled my name, and then shoved pen and paper back toward Cody.

He took them, putting them back in his backpack and getting up in one motion. It was clear this wasn't a conversation he'd wanted to have.

That made two of us.

"Does she know about me?" I asked.

"I would assume so. She had to sign this," he said, dodging the question.

"Did you know?" I asked.

Cody stopped then, and looked at me, just a quick side glance, but his face was wreathed in shame.

"Cody Larson, you knew about this and you never told me? Warned me?" I asked, hearing my voice raise.

"This was confidential," he began. "Derek was my cli—"

"Your buddy that you covered for," I said, clutching my coffee cup in one hand, coming around the island toward him. "You knew, and you did this to us! To me, and to the kids!"

"No, it wasn't like that!" he said, moving quickly out of the kitchen and toward the hall.

I followed, my hand gripping the cup so tightly that it made my arm hurt. "Get out. If there's any other business that you need to conduct with this family, you send someone else. I never want to see you again," I said.

"Come on, Wynter, please—"

"Get out, Cody," I said again, my voice hard and icy. My anger threatened to overwhelm me.

"I didn't want to hurt you," Cody said, his hands raised, palm out, in front of him.

That was it. I threw the coffee mug at him, at his lying, excuse-laden head and he had to duck as it hit the doorframe behind him.

"Wynter!" Cody had the nerve to sound offended as he stood up, one hand covering the top of his head.

"Get out," I said, my voice even softer.

He fled. The inner door shut behind him, and then I heard the outer door slam and his steps off the porch.

I thought a lot of bad words, directed at Derek. Cody. Natalie. All of them.

I didn't know how long I stood there, clenching my fists and my teeth. Then I went back into the kitchen and called the spa to cancel my appointment. I left a message for Shelly, and told her I'd call in her a couple of days. I was in no place to lie quietly on a table today, or talk to anyone else, or do anything that required me to be polite.

I stormed upstairs into our bedroom, walking into Derek's closet. We'd remodeled when the kids went to college to give ourselves each a walk in. I hadn't been able to move his clothes, still wanting to pretend he was there, to walk into his closet and smell the fresh scent of him. He always smelled like warm sunshine and sandalwood soap. Now I stared at all his clothes. The clothes of a liar. Of a cheater. Of way more than a cheater.

"Liar!" I screamed. "Liar!" I yanked at the hangers, tossing his clothing to the floor, stomping on it, pulling and tearing, not caring if I did any damage. When most of his clothing had been dumped into the growing pile, I glared at it. "You're a liar, Derek Chastain." Then I closed the closet door.

Later, next week maybe, I'd get someone to come in here, clean out the closet, and give myself a dressing room, with a vanity, a jewelry station, or whatever the hell I wanted. Right now, I never wanted to see any of his things again.

Even though it was the middle of the day, I slid off my shoes, took off my tee shirt and capris, and eased into bed, pulling the blankets up to my face. As I closed my eyes, the tears flowed.

That lying bastard. He'd ruined everything.

CHAPTER TWO

a week later, during which Cody tried to call, my kids tried to call, Shelly tried to call, and I ignored them all, I finally got out of bed. I'd spent the last week sleeping and crying, getting up only to get water or go to the bathroom. I had no will for anything else. Bad enough that I'd lost my husband. I'd just lost him all over again. Worse, he'd made sure that it was as painful as possible. How could he have kept this from me? How could I have missed this? How had he hidden an entire family?

These were all questions that needed to be answered even as the the thought of them made me exhausted.

I'd fended off the kids even though Cody had called them, telling them that they needed to talk to me. He hadn't told them why I was so upset, the weasel. No, he'd left that to me. So I'd had to promise my kids that today, they could come over, and I'd tell them everything I knew.

That meant I had to clean up, clean the house, and see what I could learn before they got here. They'd be here after lunch. Kris and Theo only lived an hour away, but Rachel was over two hours. So we'd made it just after lunchtime to make it easier for her to get here.

I took myself to the shower, and used up all the hot water before I got out. Not like anyone else was using it. I stalked past the closed door of Derek's closet. Calling a junk removal place was next, I reminded myself. I certainly wasn't going to clear out his stuff. Never again.

Cleaning up from a week of neglect didn't take long, surprisingly. Since I hadn't left my room, there wasn't much to do. Although I did take the vase of flowers, now looking a bit wilted, and march them to the trash cans out back. The lying hypocrite. It felt good to bang the lid down on the trash can so that I'd never have to see the bouquet again. After I was done, I cut up a salad, put together the fixings for sandwiches, and made iced tea for everyone. We'd agreed on after lunchtime, but I knew my kids. Someone would be hungry. Then I made myself a cup of my favorite hot tea, the Prince of Wales blend, and sat down at the kitchen table with my laptop. Time to find Natalie Chastain.

It was easy. She was on social media. She lived in Phoenix. Right there, in Arizona. and she posted lots of pictures of herself, with her kids, and with Derek.

Derek had pestered me for years to move out there, to be closer to him, and then all of a sudden, he'd stopped asking.

This might be why. In fact, I was sure Natalie was the reason why. He didn't need me there. He had her. A whole other life.

The tears streamed down my face unchecked as I scrolled through the pictures Natalie Chastain had posted. They looked happy. He didn't look like a two-timing liar who'd stolen security and a future from his wife, and his three oldest kids.

Their kids were cute, and fairly young. The oldest, a girl, couldn't have been more than nine or ten. Both she and her brother had dark blond hair, and their mother's eyes, along with their father's chin.

Natalie was cute, too. Where I was petite and blond, she was taller, with dark hair and dark, laughing eyes. She looked like someone who always had a tan because she was always outside hiking or doing something outdoorsy. They were attractive like our family was attractive.

I cried some more.

She couldn't have known. Not to be posting things like this, like they were a happy family. She couldn't have known. The thought that she might have was as painful as what my husband had done.

Thank god I'd already sold the business, I thought. It was mine and Derek's and after he was gone, I had no interest in it. I sold it to another tour operation that wanted to get into helicopter tours, and didn't look back. But if I hadn't—would I have been dealing with fights over the business as well? Could I still be facing that?

Is that why Derek had changed his policy? Because he knew I would get the business? That I'd be all right, even though it would be tough? Because our kids were nearly grown?

That didn't excuse him, I thought angrily. It hadn't been what we agreed on. We hadn't agreed on him building another family, either.

I glanced at the pictures of the smiling family again. They were cute, but until I knew this woman couldn't hurt me or my kids, I couldn't afford to be sentimental. Derek had done this to me, to us.

Getting up, I went to the sink and splashed water on my face. "No more tears," I said out loud. "No more tears for someone who did this to us. He's gotten more than enough tears over the past six months." Wiping my face, I turned around and went to the fridge. While I'd made lunch, basically, I thought it might be a long day. And that meant more food was necessary. I focused on my fridge and the pantry, glad to have something else to think about right now.

*T*he kids all came piling through the front door. "Mom!" I heard.

"In here," I called out.

Rachel, my middle child, and my only girl, came in, followed by Kris, and then Theo, the oldest. He was twenty-four, Rachel twenty-three, and Kris twenty-two. I hated to have to tell them what had happened, but at least they were grown.

"All right, Mom," Rachel said. "What's going on?"

I stifled a smile despite the reason they were here. Rachel had always been the spokesperson, keeping the peace between her brothers.

"Well, I got some news about Dad, and even though I don't want to, I have to tell you." I looked at all three of them, still innocent, still trusting, and cursed Derek Chastain.

"Your dad left some things behind that we have to talk about," I began, as I sent up a prayer to whatever deity might be listening that I didn't screw this up.

This would change everything for my kids.

Damn Derek Chastain straight to hell.

The next afternoon, I closed the front door after waving goodbye to the kids, falling against it in exhaustion. The day that they'd spent with me had been the longest day of my life. Having to explain it all to the kids, having to admit I'd had no idea, and show them the little I knew—exhausting didn't even begin to cover it. I'd cursed Derek more than once during the time the kids were here, although not out loud. The three of them had more than enough anger at what their father had done. They didn't need me adding to it.

"How could you not have known, Mom?" Theo asked. "How did he manage to hide all this?"

I shrugged, feeling small and foolish. "I don't know," I said as I wrapped my arms around myself. "I keep asking myself that, and I'll have to go back and look. Because I don't know how he managed it."

"It doesn't matter," Rachel said, her voice hard. "This isn't Mom's fault, Theo," she glared at her older brother.

"I didn't say it was," Theo protested. "But he hid an entire family for what, years? And no one knew?"

"There were some people in his circle who knew," I said, and I cringed at the bitter tone of my voice as I thought of Cody.

"Who?" All three kids cried out at once.

I told them about my meeting with Cody, and what he'd said. Rachel and Kris both cussed him, his ancestry, and his future with great vehemence. Theo sat back on the couch with his arms crossed, glaring at the fireplace.

"What does she look like?" Rachel asked abruptly.

I didn't respond right away.

"C'mon, Mom, I know you've looked her up already," Rachel said impatiently.

"How do you know that?" Kris asked.

"I would," Theo said. "Wouldn't you?"

Silently, I opened my laptop and showed them what I'd found. They scrolled through her social media quietly.

What was interesting was when they saw the many pictures of Natalie's kids—their half-siblings—all three of them had become a lot less angry. They had the same reaction I did. The kids looked like their dad, and the kids were cute. These kids, for better or worse, were their family.

I'd told them that I'd keep them updated as I learned anything, and I'd done my best to shove them out the door without shoving them out the door. I wanted to be alone.

Now, thankfully, my house was quiet, and it was just me. I pushed off from the door and went to the kitchen, absently cleaning as I thought.

My whole life had been my husband and my family. The pressures of raising a family with a spouse gone six months of the year, and making sure the business stayed in the black, and then my parents aging meant that I didn't have a lot of time for me, for friends. Although that sounded sad when I thought about it, it wasn't. I liked being alone, liked being on my own. My group of friends outside of Shelly were not close. And I loved my kids to the moon and back, but I didn't want their anger swirling around the house. Not right now. I had my hands full with my own anger.

Besides, they all needed to get back to their lives. I'd seen that need war with their concern for me. They'd stayed with me last night, refusing to leave, all heading to their old rooms, refusing to argue with me about it any longer. I thought it was good for them as well, because they needed to process how our reality had just shifted. It was different for them. Derek was their dad, and always would be. I couldn't tell them how the last week of grieving had shut down my feelings about him. They weren't ready for that. They might never be. But he would always be their dad, and they had to find a way to make peace with that. I didn't want them to carry their anger forever. His actions didn't deserve to impact them like that.

Getting back to some semblance of normal was what we all needed to do. We'd been grieving the past six months, and this would be another piece of that grief, but I wasn't going to let it eat me up, and I'd do what I could for my kids as well. They deserved better.

And deep down, I knew I'd need to reach out to Natalie, to the other wife. I could see my kids wanted to know their siblings, even if they weren't ready to say so.

But contacting Natalie could wait. No, now, I needed to take the time I'd never taken for myself over the last twenty-five years. I needed to celebrate my birthday, a week gone at this point, and do something for myself.

But what? I sat at the island, turning over ideas in my head. In the end, the simplest answer is often the best.

I was going out.

I took a long shower, and spent even longer in my closet, debating what to wear. I felt dangerous and reckless. Eventually, I decided on a pale, sea foam green dress that lapped around my knees in small, flirty curls. It was a halter dress, and as I eyed myself in the mirror from all angles, I could see that my arms didn't look too flabby, or pale. I pulled my hair into a loose chignon, put on some silver hoops, and my favorite lipstick.

I was ready. At least, I hoped I was ready. My hands were sweaty as I got into the car service I'd called. I didn't want to take the chance of driving home after drinking, even if it was only a ten-minute walk. Ten minutes was still ten minutes in the shoes I chose for tonight.

"Here you are," the young woman driving me said, glancing back in the rear view mirror. "You look great. Have a good time tonight."

"Thanks," I said, smiling for the first time in over a week. "I'm going to try."

"You're ready for it," she laughed.

I got out, waving as she drove away. I left her a big tip on the app. She must have known that I needed a boost, even from a stranger.

God, hopefully that didn't show up all over me in neon lights.

The Black Dog Bar and Grille loomed in front of me. I took a breath, and walked in. I knew they had a DJ, and I'd done a little searching online to see where people would be.

I didn't want to be alone tonight.

What that meant, specifically, I didn't know. All I did know was that I wanted to be around other people who didn't know me, who didn't know the Chastain family, and wouldn't look at me with pity. It was silly to assume that everyone knew—but that's how I felt. That everyone but me knew. I mean, had Cody been able to keep his mouth shut? He certainly had with me, but who knew if he'd told anyone else?

The bar was dimly lit and I relaxed a little. I could see groups of people, but no one I knew. Good. I walked down the bar, and when I saw four empty seats, I took the third one, leaning against the bar as I slid onto the chair.

"What can I get you?" The bartender, a young man in black with an easy, knowing grin, tossed a drink napkin in front of me. "We have an amazing sparkling Sangria, house recipe. I'm just saying."

"That's perfect," I said.

He grinned again and whirled away. Within moments, I had a glass in front of me sending out the delicious scent of orange. I sipped it. The bartender was right. It was amazing.

Drink in hand, I turned to watch the action at the bar. It was Thursday night, and since we were at the end of summer, Thursdays were still busy. I didn't recognize anyone I knew, but that made sense. Locals tended to stay home during the summer months.

Several men walked by, making eye contact, but I looked down. Not yet. Maybe not at all.

After I'd been there a while—my glass was half empty —someone sat down on the bar stool next to me, his clothing all beige and neutral. He set a hat—leather, Indiana Jones style—on the bar. "Can I get an Offshore Islander?" he asked, naming a beer from a local brewery. He glanced over at me. "Is anyone sitting here? I can move, if so." He put his hand on his hat.

I looked over at him then. His face was tanned, as though he'd spent his life in the sun. He had a five o'clock shadow, although on this guy I'd say he had more like a ten o'clock stubble. His grin was easy, his teeth white in the darkness of the bar. His shirt was open two buttons to show a tanned chest and every-thing about him said, *adventure*.

Something clicked in me. Perfect.

"Well, yes, there is," I said, smiling. "You are." He even looked like Indiana Jones, and that was not a bad thing at all.

He stared at me as though he couldn't believe what he was seeing. His mouth fell open a little, and he looked dazed.

I hoped I didn't have something off about me. I'd checked myself in the mirror at least a thousand times before I left. I hadn't ordered anything to eat at the bar. There couldn't be food in my teeth.

Then he blinked, seeming to come back from wherever he'd been for a couple of seconds. His grin widened. "Ashton Flint, but you can call me Ash," he said, sticking out a hand.

I took it. "Wynter Chastain," I said.

He lifted my hand to his lips, his eyes never leaving mine as his lips brushed against my skin. "Delighted," he murmured.

I felt my skin flush and my body heated in ways I didn't expect to feel. Well, what can you say when one of your childhood movie crushes walks off the screen and shows up in front of you after the worst week of your life?

To hell with it. I was going to enjoy tonight, and Mr. Ashton Flint, dead ringer for Indiana Jones.

"I haven't seen you around here," I said. "Are you on vacation?"

Ash's eyes flicked around the bar in a wary manner, but his face relaxed into a smile when he looked at me. "No, I've been traveling for work."

"You look it," I said, looking down at his dusty looking clothing.

"I was traipsing all over sand dunes today. I'm surprised I'm not trailing it behind me," he said with a laugh.

"What do you do?" I asked.

"Oh, I'm a knockabout," he said. "I do a little of this, a little of that. Tonight, however, I'm celebrating. It's been a good week for me."

Knockabout. That was a word my dad used to use, and it felt slightly old fashioned. "Really? Why so good?" I asked.

Ash's eyes moved around the bar. He looked wary. Then he looked down at me and his features relaxed. "I finally… reached a goal I've been working on for a long time," he said.

"That's really satisfying," I said, gazing up at him.

"You have no idea," he said, his hand brushing mine as he picked up his beer. "It's been a long time."

"Then let's celebrate," I said, pleased to have someone else to focus on.

We talked more, flirting madly, until Ash set his bottle of beer on the bar. "Would you like to dance?" He looked at me directly, not even trying to hide the appreciation in his gaze.

"Yes," I said, getting up. I liked the way he looked at me—like he was lucky to have met me. It had been a while since anyone looked at me in that way. And even then, I reminded myself, it wasn't real. I pushed that thought aside and focused on being in the moment, in the here and now.

When Ash took my hand in his, I felt a spark, a jump of electricity from him to me. I shot a look at him, but he didn't look down as he led me to the dance floor. Was it possible I was the only one feeling this?

No. I couldn't be.

I wrapped my arms around his neck and leaned into him. Ash was a skilled dancer, leading me carefully among the other dancers. His body felt good next to mine, and I inhaled his scent of sun, sweat, and soap.

We danced for what felt like hours. The lights in the bar flashed, and it was as though we were in a dream. Ash would occasionally look down at me as his hand curled mine next to his chest, and my blood kept racing like I was running sprints.

What was happening?

I didn't care. This felt wonderful.

"Would you like to come back to my room for a drink?" Ash murmured into my ear. "I love dancing with you, but it's loud in here."

I blinked, staring at his chest. Did I want to? I knew what this meant. Well, what it might mean. I might be assuming too much. Taking a deep breath, I looked up at him and smiled. "Let's go," I said.

"It's not a long walk. I have a room at the Oak Bluffs Inn," Ash murmured.

We walked through the downtown area, his arm around me, bringing me close as we passed people on the sidewalk. I liked it, the feeling of being cared for.

A dark van raced past us, faster than normal for the traffic downtown, and Ash's arm tightened around my waist. "We're almost there," he said.

Sweet baby Jee. The reality of what was happening, what I was allowing to happen, hit me. I hoped I didn't know the person at the front desk of the Inn. I hadn't even thought about being busted. I wasn't really close to anyone outside of Shelly anymore, but I'd lived here my entire life. I knew the people of the town. I crossed my fingers behind my back and hoped for the best.

There was no one in the lobby, and Ash led me up the stairs to the third floor taking them at almost a run. I liked that he was so full of life. He opened the door to his room, and I walked in. Ash came behind me, wrapping an arm around my waist as the door closed. He bent down to nuzzle my neck. "I love this up do," he said, his fingers trailing through tendrils of my hair that had fallen down around my neck.

The room was a small apartment, with an open living area and kitchenette. It overlooked the town, and the lights twinkled merrily outside. It was charming.

I turned around and reached up to put my arms around his neck. He was at least a foot taller, but he bent down to kiss me. His lips felt like the first time I'd taken his hand—an electric shock that was more than just mere sexual attraction. His hands moved into my hair, pulling at the pins as he kissed me hungrily.

I found that I responded to him, although I had the nagging feeling it was more than just my Indy-come-to-life that I was responding to.

Ash, still kissing me, began walking me backward toward the bedroom.

"Just a sec," I managed to gasp. "May I use the bathroom?" The feeling of rising heat had knocked me right out my haze. A hot flash was coming. Mine tended to start at my feet, and then move up my body. As well, this—whatever this was—this thing with Ash was moving fast. What had I expected? I didn't know, but I needed a minute, or five.

"Sure," his grin was easy. "Right through there." He pointed opposite of the bedroom door. "I'll be waiting," he added, walking to the bedroom and unbuttoning his shirt.

I fled to the bathroom, locking the door behind me. Looking in the mirror, my hair was a wreck, and my face was flushed. My lips were swollen, and my eyes were bright. Basically, a glorious mess. If I ignored my bright pink face.

Yep, hot flash.

Well, if I was going to be with the second man in my life ever, I was going to do it right. I took down my hair, using my fingers to comb it out. I ran the water and washed my face, patting down my chest with cool water as well. I slipped off my shoes, and sat on the edge of the tub, running the cool water over my feet, so that I felt less sweaty and awkward and old.

There was a loud crash from outside of the bathroom.

"Are you all right?" I called out.

There was no answer. It must be someone else in the hotel. I finished my ablutions, and then smiled at myself in the mirror, grabbing my shoes and purse. Looking in the mirror one last time, I smiled. "Happy birthday to me," I said. I might be a week late, but a celebration was a celebration. And this marked the beginning of a new phase of life for me. Happy birthday, indeed.

Then I opened the door and walked out.

CHAPTER THREE

I took two steps into the open living area, and my mouth fell open. The room was trashed. All of the drawers in the kitchenette were pulled open, their contents spilled out onto the floor. The couch had been knocked forward on its face, and I could see the lining along the bottom had been split. The easy chair by the window had a large slash along the seat as well. Had a knife done that? The horror in me grew and blossomed. Was someone still here? With a knife?

"Ash?" I said in a half-whisper. What had happened? How had this happened in the five minutes I'd been in the bathroom? Oh, shit. Was the person or people who'd done this still here? Where was Ash? I dropped down, clutching my purse to me. Shit, shit, shit. I looked around wildly. This had seemed like such a good idea two minutes ago. "Ash?" I whispered again.

On my hands and knees, I crawled toward the bedroom. There was no one there. The hat that Ash had been wearing was on the floor.

"Mother of Pearl," I whispered. I stayed crouched down for some time, listening, jumping every time I heard anything. What in the name of all that was holy had happened? And how did I keep myself safe?

I needed to call the police. That much I knew. I got up, putting my shoes on. *Think, Wynter, think.* It figured. I went out for the first time in years, and ended up in a room with a guy who disappeared under the most scary of circumstances.

Which wasn't very nice of me, since I was here and fine. What had happened to Ash? God, I hoped he was all right. I tottered over to the slashed easy chair and sat down. As I dropped into the chair, I yelped. "What the hell?"

Something hard and sharp dug into my thigh. I reached underneath me, my hand sliding into the slashed section of the cushion where the thing had dug into me. My hand met metal, and I closed my fingers around it and pulled it out.

It was a bracelet, shaped like a serpent. It was bright gold, so bright that it had to be fake. The eyes of the serpent were a glittering white, sparkling and shining.

"Wow," I said. The scales of the serpent were well-defined, and they ran along the entire length of the bracelet.

As though there were a voice in my head directing me, I slid it onto my wrist. It looked good against my skin, even though it was loose. I move it up to my forearm where it fit more snugly. "Wow," I said again. This was one of those armbands like you'd see in a museum, snugly wrapped around some woman's arm. I couldn't believe I was playing around with a piece of jewelry in what was the middle of someone else's absolute disaster, but the heavy gold felt warm and right on my forearm. It was beautiful, and it fit perfectly. I'd always thought the armband bracelets would be uncomfortable, but this felt... right.

The eyes of the snake sparkled, brighter and brighter until I had to put my hand over my eyes. "What the—" I began.

The white light shrouded my vision and I knew no more.

*W*hen my eyes opened, the first thing I noticed was that my neck was sore. Which was probably because I was still in the easy chair with my head flung back against the back edge of the chair. "Ow," I said, carefully sitting up and rubbing my neck.

The bracelet! Where was it? I looked all over, but it was gone.

"Ash?" I called out.

There was no answer. I was alone.

Okay, this night was getting weirder and weirder. I would have thought I was dreaming except I was still in the trashed living room in Ash's hotel room. This was too much. I'd had enough. "Okay, I'm done. I'm going home. The bracelet is all yours. Good night," I said. The forearm where I'd tried on the bracelet ached suddenly, and I rubbed at it. It felt strange, almost as though I was still wearing the bracelet.

Which was silly, but I wanted to let whatever—whoever —know that I was out of their business once and for all. I sent up a prayer to whomever it was that looked out for knockabouts that Ash was all right.

"Oh, god," I whispered. "Ash." Where was he? Was he hurt? Or worse? I tried to stand up, and my legs gave out. I collapsed back into the ruined chair, my head spinning.

I woke up, rubbing my eyes and trying to remember what the hell happened.

Get up, a light, airy-sounding voice said.

"Who's there?" I sat up, ignoring the ache of my back and between my shoulder blades. This whole exercise in proving I could take bad news was making a left turn in the wrong direction. Way wrong.

Get up, and get out of here. You cannot tarry, the voice said.

"Who are you?"

I will appear to you once the first consultant arrives seeking counsel. Until then, you must keep yourself safe. The voice went silent then, and even though I waited, said nothing more.

My right forearm still ached terribly. I looked down. It was pink, and in the light, it almost looked… metallic.

I shook my head. Weird. This whole thing was weird, and a bad idea, and just showed me why I needed to skip solo wine night for the rest of my life.

I got up, and walked around the suite. Something had clearly happened while I was in the bathroom. Thank god nothing happened while I was passed out in the chair. I sighed. I couldn't leave things like this, much as I wanted to just run away and forget I'd ever had the idea to go out on the town. I pulled out my phone and dialed the number for Oak Bluffs Police Department.

Twelve minutes later, after I'd checked my phone at least a thousand times, two officers knocked on the partially open door. I was still in the chair with the torn seat. Before I'd come out of the bathroom, I'd been sweating like crazy. Now I was cold, and wishing that I'd brought a wrap. I didn't want to touch anything in the room, so I sat on the chair and shivered.

Andy Dentwhistle, someone I'd known since childhood, walked closer to me. He looked very official in his uniform, and very stern. Andy removed his hat, running his hand through his light red hair. "Wynter, what are you doing here?"

"I was the one who called this in," I said, feeling a little stung.

He glanced at his partner, and then back to me. "What happened?"

"I came up here with my friend Ash to have a drink. I stepped into the bathroom, and when I came out, the room was like this."

"You didn't touch anything?" the other officer asked. His eyes were narrow, and his face was far more suspicious than Andy's.

"I sat down," I said, gesturing at the seat. "I didn't know what else to do."

"Did you search the room?" the second officer asked.

"I called out for Ash, and looked in the bedroom, but he wasn't there."

"You didn't hear anything in the bathroom?" Andy looked around. "This is a pretty big mess."

"I had the water running," I said. "I didn't hear anything."

Neither officer said anything.

Finally, Andy broke the silence. "Well, let's get all the details. And maybe you can give us an idea of what this Ash character looks like."

"I don't really know anything," I said. The enormity of what I'd stepped in was hitting me. I'd been Wynter Chastain, PTA mom and all around good person. Now I was in a B & B, obviously tarted up and out on the town, with a guy that it was going to be clear I didn't know much about.

Oak Bluffs was a small town. I was going right into the gossip mill. Do not pass Go. Do not collect two hundred dollars. I'd be there until the town chewed me up, or someone more scandalous came along.

Mother of Pearl.

"Wynter, I'm going to go call this in. My partner Scott will start getting some information from you," Andy said.

"Scott Trenton," Scott said, his tone all business. He perched on the overturned couch across from me. "What's Ash's full name?"

"Ashton Flint," I said.

"How old is he?"

"I don't know," I replied. "Maybe in his forties?"

Scott nodded as he wrote in a small notebook, not looking up. "And is he from around here?"

"I don't know," I said. "I just met him."

"Tonight?" Scott looked up then, one eyebrow raised.

"Yes," I said, not looking away. I would not be shamed by this guy, even though I could feel my cheeks getting warm.

"So you didn't know him before tonight?" Scott asked.

I shook my head. "No. I—" I stopped.

"What is it?" Scott leaned forward.

"I don't know. I went out to get out of the house. He was sitting next to me at the bar—"

"Which bar?" Scott interrupted.

"The Black Dog Bar and Grille," I said.

"Can anyone verify you were at the bar?" Scott asked.

"The bartender," I said.

"Was that where you met Mr. Flint? Sitting at the bar?" He looked up at me then.

"Yes," I said.

"Was anyone unhappy with him that you could see? At the bar?" He was writing in his notebook again.

"No," I said. "We were talking and dancing. I didn't see anyone give him any trouble, or anything at all," I said.

"How much did you have to drink, Mrs. Chastain?" he asked. He looked up again.

"Um…" I had to think about it. "Two glasses of sangria."

"Nothing else?" He looked at my face.

"No," I said. I wondered if it was still bright pink.

"No drugs?"

"No," I said again, more forcefully.

Then Andy came back in. "Christine, our forensics tech, is on her way over. What have you got so far?" He stopped next to Scott.

Scott showed him the notebook, and for a moment, neither of the men spoke as they read Scott's notes.

"So you don't really know this guy?" Andy asked me.

"No," I said, remembering to meet his gaze and not look away. "We'd just met. He seemed very nice. He said he was a knockabout," I said. "He also said he'd been all over the sand dunes today."

"Doing what?" Scott asked.

I shrugged. "I don't know. He didn't share that with me."

They continued to question me, with the questions taking on a suspicious bent. When I heard another knock at the door, I was relieved. Because I was starting to get pissed.

A woman stuck her head in. "Can I come in?"

"Sure," Andy waved her in. "Christine Savoy, our tech. Go on," he said to Christine. "We're almost done." He looked back at me. "You'll need to come down to the station with us."

"Why?" I sat up straight. "I haven't done anything wrong."

"You were the last person to see a man who is now missing," Scott began.

Andy stopped him with a hand. "I need you to work with our sketch artist, Wynter, and give us an idea of who to look for."

I sighed. "All right," I said. "I don't have a choice, do I?"

"No," Scott said, before Andy could speak. "Let's go."

I got up, gathering my purse, and followed the two officers out the door. This was so much worse than I expected.

On the main floor, an older woman, Hazel Babbington, the owner, stood at the reception desk. Andy veered off to speak to her, and Scott moved closer.

"Come out to the car. Where are you parked?"

"I got a ride-share downtown," I said.

He nodded.

Walking out the door, I saw Hazel glance at me with wide, intense eyes. The gossip train was already rolling out of the station.

Scott led me to the patrol car, and opened the back seat.

"Oh, god," I muttered. I'd never been in a police car in my life, and now I was riding in the back.

Like a suspect.

Scott got into the passenger side, and a few moments later, Andy came out of the hotel. He got in the driver's side without speaking and started the car.

This was worse than I expected. I sighed, then inhaled deeply. Even if I didn't want to, I had to do the right thing. Which was exactly what I'd done. If that meant I'd be the prime source of gossip for a while, so be it, even as the thought made my skin itch. Although I wasn't sure why I cared. I was widowed. I had no ties. I had even less ties than I'd thought I had. I was free, over twenty-one, and not dead.

But that didn't stop the shame.

My face was hot as I walked between Andy and Scott into the police station. They brought me to a small room with ugly blue walls, and one table with four chairs around it.

"Have a seat," Andy said. "We have a few more questions, and I'll get the sketch artist on their way."

"All right," I said, trying to keep my impatience in check.

An hour later, I lost the battle. "I've been here an hour, and there's nothing else I can tell you," I said, my patience totally gone.

Andy and Scott had questioned me over and over, asking the same thing in different ways. Thirty minutes ago, a young man with a sketch pad had come in, and while they continued to question me, he was busily creating a picture.

At my words, William, the young man who was doing the sketch looked up, alarmed.

"We just need to make sure," Andy began.

"No. You have made sure more than once already, Andy. I don't know what is going on, but William and I have been over this sketch multiple times, and I don't have anything more to offer," I said. I got up. "I would like to leave now."

Scott came over to stand behind Andy, his eyes cold.

Andy was quiet, watching me. "You can go," he said finally. "But don't leave town, Wynter."

"Excuse me?" I said. I mean, I knew this was coming, from the moment Scott Suspicious Trenton started in with his questions. I just didn't want to believe it. Now we were here.

I was, in fact, a suspect.

"You heard me. Come on, I'll take you home," Andy said.

"No, thank you," I lifted my chin. "I can get myself home."

"Wynter—" Andy started.

I spun on my heel and walked away. I was done with this place, and if that meant I had to walk home, so be it.

It was only four blocks, so it wasn't like I was making a grand gesture, but as I stalked out of the police station, my head high and my back ramrod straight, I felt like it was the grandest of gestures ever made.

A block away from the station, I felt my bravado flee.

I was a suspect. Andy had been too nice to say it, but that's what I was.

Oh, my god.

I rubbed at my right forearm as I walked. It still hurt. I must have hit it when I passed out, but I didn't remember it. I sighed. It was just one more thing that had gone wrong tonight. My feet hurt from wearing heels for so long, something I didn't usually do.

And what had happened to Ash? Anything I'd been hoping for when I'd gone up to his hotel room was gone. Now I just hoped that he was okay, that nothing bad had happened. That he'd merely decided he didn't want to spend an evening with me. That would kick my pride right in the teeth, but if he was safe, I'd take it.

He'd been so pleased, jubilant even, when I'd met him in the bar.

On the way home, I passed the East China Garden restaurant. Despite the late hour, it was still open. I stopped in, and ordered Hunan scallops. It wouldn't solve all my problems, but it might make me feel better.

While I waited for my order, I was considering what could have happened to Ash, and coming to the conclusion that I understand why the police were thinking as they did when I approached my house.

As I walked up the steps to the porch, Chinese food in one hand, my other hand scrabbled in my purse for the keys. I stopped at the door to peer into it. "Where the hell are you?" I grumbled.

"It's about time," a man's voice said.

"What in the ever loving hell?" I shrieked, reaching into my purse once more and finding the small canister. The bag of food dropped to the porch. I'd always laughed about keeping my pepper spray in my purse, here in sleepy Oak Bluffs, and had done so to make Derek and the kids happy. But with one flick of my finger, I opened it and stuck out my hand, spraying the pepper spray into the hulking form that had his big ass feet on the railing of my porch.

"Ow!" he howled, loud enough to wake the entire neighborhood.

"Help! Police!" I screamed.

He's not a foe, I heard in my head. It was nothing like I'd ever heard before, and it scared the shit out of me. One more thing to scare me to death tonight.

"What?" I shouted.

Not a foe. Not a friend. He is neutral, and he isn't going to harm you, so no need to kill. The voice was matter of fact, light and airy, as though we were discussing the weather.

"Who said that?" I shouted, whirling around with the pepper spray in my hand, ready to use again.

"Could you not spray that at me again, please?"

"Who are you?" I asked, backing up to the other side of the porch.

"My name is Logan Gentry, and I've come to ask for your help," he said, rubbing his eyes. "Can I also ask for some water, for gods' sake?"

"What do you want?" I asked.

"I need the help of the Oracle," Logan Gentry said.

I could hear it then, the way he said the word 'Oracle'. It was capitalized, like a title.

"I think you have the wrong place, Mr. Gentry," I said. "I've had one of the worst nights of my life, so if you'll just get off my porch, that would be great. Otherwise, the cops will be here shortly," I added.

"Because you sprayed me with pepper without provocation?" he snapped. "And I'm not leaving. I told you. I need your help. It's taken a lot of effort for me to get here to see you."

"What? You want some water? There's a hose out in the yard," I said, impatient. "And you're trespassing."

"Water would be great, like now, but no, that's not it," he said, his jaw clenched, his eyes screwed shut. "I told you, I need the help of the Oracle."

I saw a light turn on across the street. Great. My shrieking had woken people up. I didn't need this. I eyed Logan Gentry. He was huge, with dark hair a touch too long, a scar along one cheek, and cheekbones that could cut butter. He was quite attractive, if you took the whole creeping around on a woman's porch aspect out of it.

Well, I could always spray him again. "Fine. You can come in and use the kitchen sprayer," I said, not happy about it.

"Don't kill yourself being gracious," he snapped back, raising a hand to his face.

I found my keys, unlocked the door, and stalked in. He could make his own way in. I heard his footsteps behind me, and a thud and a grunt as he banged into the inside door.

That's what you get, I thought. Shouldn't be hanging out in the dark waiting to scare innocent women. "The sink is here," I said. I walked around the island, my pepper spray still in hand.

Logan was even taller and more imposing now that I could see him than he was in the dark, if that was possible. He wore faded jeans that rode on his hips, and black cowboy boots. A black leather belt and a dark blue shirt with one button undone completed his look. He looked dangerous and capable, I thought as I watched the muscles of his shoulders move under the dark blue shirt. He was at ease with himself, comfortable in his own skin. You could see it in the way he moved. He was one with his body.

He bent over the sink, using the sprayer to flush his eyes. Then he stopped, and turned around. "I need to get under my shirt. If you don't mind?"

"No," I said, pressing myself against the back of the couch, pepper spray ready. Logan Gentry unbuttoned his shirt and shrugged out of it, letting it fall to his waist where it was still tucked into his jeans.

I had to cover my mouth to stifle a gasp.

There were small white scars all over his back and he was, in fact, as muscular and toned as I thought. He'd obviously been in an accident, or a fight, or something. Something that might not bode well for me.

I wished I had my Taser. When I carried it, it was in my bra strap, but my dress tonight had no chance of a bra. The straps on the halter certainly wouldn't support the Taser. I'd tried. So I'd tucked the pepper spray in my purse out of habit instead, never thinking I'd have to use it.

The silence in the kitchen stretched on as Logan Gentry kept washing his hands and flushing his eyes. This suggested this wasn't his first go round with pepper spray. Then he pulled his shirt out of his jeans, sliding it back on, and as he was buttoning it up, he turned to face me. His eyes were red at the moment, but they looked to be green.

Next to his light russet skin tone, it was very striking. Everything about Logan Gentry was striking. Had I not been nervous, he would have taken my breath away. But I was nervous.

"Now can we talk without you spraying me again?" he asked.

"I don't know. What is it you think I can do for you? And remember, the cops are still coming."

"So you said," Logan said, and I could hear humor in his voice.

He thought this was funny? What the hell?

"But that doesn't change the fact that you're the only one who can help me," he continued.

I threw my hands up. "I don't even know you," I said. "So how can I possibly help you?"

Logan stared at me, his mouth falling open.

Wow. He had full, dark red lips. I was busy staring at them when he spoke again.

"You are the Oracle. That's what you do. Help people who come to see you, who need your help."

"What is the Oracle?" I asked. "Can we start there?"

"You really don't know? When did you get it?" he asked.

"Get what?" I asked.

"I'm going to come closer. Please don't pepper spray me," he said. He came around the island, his hand up, palms facing me, and picked up my right arm. "This," he said, tracing along my forearm.

My entire body shivered. "What are you talking about?" My voice died as I saw what he was touching.

It was the replica of the bracelet I'd found in Ash's room. In the aftermath, I hadn't thought about it since. But now, here it was on my arm. "How did this get there?" I asked. A golden serpent, bright as though it were brand new. The scales were visible, from the head to the tail. And the eyes were bright, shining like beacons over a dark ocean.

"What is this?" I whispered, taking a step back, clutching my forearm. This… this tattoo, or mark, or whatever, hadn't been there when I'd gone out to pick up dinner. What was happening? I felt my world tilt under my feet.

"That's the mark of the Oracle. Which makes you the Oracle. So can you help me?" Logan asked.

"I… this isn't… I mean," I held my forearm as I stepped back even more, bumping into the couch. "I'm not supposed to be anything, much less an Oracle."

"But you are," Logan's face came close, swimming in front of my eyes. "What's your name? I feel weird calling you the Oracle."

"Wynter," I said, as his face swam even more. "I'm no oracle. Just plain Wynter Chastain."

At that moment, thankfully, everything around me went black, Logan's face shrinking to a small white dot. Then even he disappeared and I sank into darkness.

CHAPTER FOUR

"*H*ey, I'm sorry, I didn't mean to scare you," the man's voice said.

I'd seen this guy before. He was... who was he? Logan. That's what he called himself. He'd been waiting for me, on my porch. After I got home from being questioned by the police. Because a man I was with disappeared.

Where was I? I was in my house, on my couch. I'd come home and—Logan had been there.

I think I'd dropped my Chinese food on the porch. Damn it.

"Oh, my god," I gasped. I scooted along the couch, moving away from where he sat until I bumped into the arm, and I got up, scuttling around the side of the couch. If I timed it right, I could run through the door of the kitchen, get to my room, and lock the door behind me while I really did call the cops. "What do you want? I don't have anything. I don't have any money. There's not really any money," I said, thinking about Cody's visit last week, and started to laugh. "There's not a whole lot of anything," I got out, laughing harder.

Logan stopped, and took two steps back. "Are you all right?" His voice was wary.

I couldn't reply, but laughed even more, leaning against the doorframe of the kitchen, clutching at the frame as I bent over. It was still dark outside, meaning I hadn't been out all that long.

He just stood there. I could see dark patches along the collar of his shirt from his ablutions at the sink earlier. From the pepper spray, I remembered. If he'd wanted to hurt me, he'd had his chance. I'd already hurt him, too. So he knew I wasn't helpless. But he was so much bigger, and I was so... right in the middle of falling apart. Plenty of chances, because I was a mess, and not even able to fully breathe. When I finally caught my breath, and stood up, I said, "Okay, let's try this again. Your name is Logan, right?"

"Yes," he said, eyeing me warily. "I'm Logan Gentry." He paused. "I am, as I told you before you passed out, here seeking your counsel," he said, his tone far more formal than when he gave his name.

"Why in the hell would you want my counsel?" I asked, too tired to manage my normal level of civility. "I'm nearly broke, widowed, and now I'm a suspect in something, a disappearance," I finished. "I don't think anyone wants to hear from me." His words stirred something in me. My counsel. Where had I heard that recently?

Logan came forward, and I could see that he was as tall as I'd first thought, but he didn't look like a mass murderer. Or even a Wynter murderer. "You're the Oracle," he said. "There's no one else who can offer counsel."

The way he said it, the Oracle—I could hear the capital letter again. The Oracle was a name, to him. The same way he'd been saying it since he'd shown up.

"I have no idea what you're talking about," I said. "I'm sorry, Logan Gentry, but it's been a really long night, and I need to go to bed."

"It took me two weeks to find you," Logan said, and I could hear a note of something in his voice. Fear? Worry? Whatever it was, he didn't want to let this go.

"I didn't even get anything that felt like a response until this morning. So I came right to you."

"Well, I'm sorry. I can't help you. Now if you'll excuse me," I said, and I pulled my pepper spray out once more. How I hadn't dropped it was some sort of miracle. "Please leave, Mr. Gentry. I'd hate to have to call the police." I really would, too. God, they'd think even worse of me than they did now. I hoped my threat was sincere enough.

"No, you don't understand," Logan said.

"I understand all that I need to," I said. "I am asking you to leave. The door is that way." I pointed down the hallway toward the front door.

Logan Gentry stared at me, and I could see that frustration and desperation warred within him. It was all over his face. His full lips pressed together, and then he exhaled, a long breath that suggested he was seeking patience.

Oh, now he needed patience to deal with me?

The anger and fear and frustration that was bubbling inside of me took over. "I have asked you to leave. I don't want to ask again."

His eyes narrowed, and he literally stomped, like one of my kids, past me and down the hallway. He stopped at the vestibule door, looking over his shoulder. Then he yanked the door open, and walked through, letting it slam behind him. He managed to slam the front door as well. I waited for a moment, then ran down the hallway and locked the door.

I heard him say something, but his words were muffled by the two doors now locked and bolted between me and him. God, just let him go away.

"Well, that was one hell of a birthday celebration," I said.

How I got upstairs, and got in my pajamas, I didn't know. But my eyes were closed as my head hit the pillow. Maybe tomorrow, this would all look better. I'd hoped I'd be able to rest, to refresh.

Instead, I dreamed.

I dreamed about a book. It was big and old and a dark greenish brown color, like old leather. There were metal hinges on one side, and a metal hasp on the other. It looked like something you'd see in a movie. It was glowing, and sparkling, and I wanted nothing more than to touch it. There were things in the background, but my vision was full of this book, and I couldn't pay attention to anything else. My hand, in the dream, was reaching out for it. I wanted to touch it, to lay my hand on the cover, feel the leather and metal work. Just as my hand hovered over the book, a light like the sun obscured my vision. It was similar to when I'd put the bracelet on, and the light from the serpent's eyes blinded me. But unlike then, I wasn't scared. I didn't pass out. I was... happy.

Okay. It was weird to feel so happy, so content. The last week had been miserable, and here in my dream, the thought of a book, this book specifically, made my life seem better in all ways.

"Where are you?" I asked out loud. There was no answer to my question, but the light that obscured everything else was dimming, allowing me to see.

You must find it, the airy voice I'd heard before said.

"What? How?" I asked.

The book was still there, in front of me.

And then I saw nothing more.

When I opened my eyes again, it was morning. I stretched, enjoying the silence of the house and the sun streaming through the curtains across from me. I was warm and comfy—then I remembered last night.

"Oh, god," I groaned, and I rolled over into my pillow. Ash. The bracelet. The police. Logan. I must have fallen back asleep because the next thing I knew, I was sitting up in bed, my heart pounding like I'd run a marathon, and the doorbell ringing.

"Oh, no," I whispered. Had I forgotten something? I scrambled out of bed, tossing on a robe, and pulling my hair into a scrunchie. A splash of water on the face, a chug of mouthwash, and I raced down the stairs.

Whoever was at the door was persistent. Probably the police, I thought, thinking of the intense look on Officer Scott Trenton's face. Think positive, think positive. Maybe they'd found Ash. Oh, I hoped so. I'd put up with Scott Trenton looking at me like I'd just stolen the crown jewels if they could tell me they'd found Ash alive and well.

My guilt raced through me, making me feel hot and uncomfortable. Unfortunately, it was solid guilt, and not a hot flash. I'd only just met him, but I didn't want him to be hurt. My mind still on Ash, I opened the door.

"Hello," said a large man. He was tall, very tall. His hair came down to his shoulders, slightly wavy and dark, and his skin had a warm, reddish hue that made me think of days lived in the sun. He wore faded jeans that hung just right on his hips, and a dark blue shirt with one button undone. I could see his muscled physique even in these casual clothes. He radiated power, and something very physical. His lips were full, his mouth wide, his cheekbones high—but his green eyes were serious, and his brows lowered as he gazed down at me with what could only be called a worried expression. "Are you ready to talk to me? Because I really need your help. There is no one else who can help me."

I clutched at my tee shirt, feeling very exposed under his gaze. "Who are you?" I asked, even as I thought I should know him. My brain felt fuzzy and unable to hold even a single thought.

He rolled his eyes then, taking a step back. "Haven't we been over this? Like, more than once?" He glared.

I glared back.

He sighed. "You're the Oracle. I've been waiting to talk to you for two weeks. I've been doing the fire ceremony every night, and finally I was given your location. When I did find you, you pepper sprayed me and then threw me out of your house."

Oh, yeah. Last night was coming back to me, even more clearly than I wanted. "What—" I began, and then a pain shot through my right forearm that was so strong I fell against the door frame.

Logan, I thought through the waves of pain. Logan Gentry. That was his name, or at least the name he gave me last night. Holy hell. I did pepper spray him. I looked up at him, trying to focus. Had he been sitting on my porch all night? What were my neighbors going to say? "Where is the food?"

"What?"

"I dropped food last night when you scared me." Why hadn't I gone out to find it?

"Oh," his face relaxed. "I picked it up, and ate it."

"What?" Right now, cold Chinese food sounded great. And he'd eaten it. My indignation fled as the pain from my arm shot through me again. My fingernails dug into my hand as I tried to breathe through it. I hadn't read about hot flashes having this sort of effect. What was happening to me?

Oh, god. Was I having a heart attack? A stroke?

The worried look in his face intensified. "Are you all right?" He reached down for me, his hands on my arms to steady me.

"No, please," I began, trying to back up.

I took a few steps back into the house, and then stumbled, falling backwards and landing on my butt. Great.

At least I was wearing pajama bottoms, and not a nightgown.

"Are you sure you're the Oracle?" Logan asked as he bent down and helped me to stand. "I've never asked for help from the Oracle before, but you don't seem very together." He stopped, his expression shifting. "I'm sorry, I'm not trying to be rude."

"Well, you are," I said, pushing myself away from him. "Rude, that is. I have no idea what you're talking about. I'm no oracle. I'm just..." I stopped, not wanting to give him my name. What if he was not only crazy, but a stalker of some sort?

"Of course you're the Oracle," he said, and I could hear the difference again, like I had last night, in the way he said the word 'oracle'. "You have the mark, Wynter."

"What?" I took another step into my house. " What mark? How do you know my name?"

"The mark is right there, on your arm," Logan spoke slowly as he pointed at my right forearm. "I know your name because you told me last night."

"I don't have a—" I stopped as I looked down. There, on my forearm, which had been burning and uncomfortable since... oh, my god. Since last night. When I tried on the bracelet. When I blacked out. When the bracelet disappeared, and then my arm was weird looking. The mark was there last night, too. I felt like I was in some kind of crazy repeat nightmare. This was everything that had happened last night, but during the day time, which made it harder to ignore.

There on my arm was an exact replica of the serpent bracelet I'd tried on. It even had the glittery look of the scales that I'd so admired last night.

"How is this possible?" I whispered, my hand brushing carefully against the image.

I told you I'd appear when your first consultant came to you. And so he has, seeking your counsel, the light, thin voice I'd heard last night said.

"Who are you?" I asked. That was where I'd heard about someone seeking counsel—from the voice last night. And now from Logan Gentry.

"I'm Logan Gentry," the man in front of me said, sounding annoyed. "For the tenth or hundredth time."

"Not you," I waved my hand at him. "Where are you?" I whirled around, ignoring the pain in my arm. I recognized that light, airy voice. All mystical and not telling me a thing.

There was no answer.

I turned back to Logan. "Okay, what is the deal? What do you want?"

"Can I come in? I really don't want to stand out here and discuss this with you," he said. He looked annoyed, too. "We've gone over this, but if you need to hear it again, I suppose I can do that."

The nerve. He sounded all sorts of put out.

"Discuss what? What in the world do we have to discuss?" I asked.

"Woman, I'm losing my patience," he said, his voice coming out in growl. He moved closer to me.

I didn't have my pepper spray, darn it. Holding out my hands, even though my right arm was screaming in pain, I said, "I don't care what you're losing. I didn't and I'm not inviting you in."

Logan stopped. "I've been waiting out here all night. I can't leave until I speak with you. I even put up with you spraying me, which no one does." He looked at me, and then made a decision. "If you don't want to talk to me, fine. But I'm not leaving until you change your mind. So, I'll just be out here." He grinned, which was unexpected, and it transformed his entire face. Then he pivoted on his heel and went over to one of the wicker chairs, dropping into it. The chair creaked as he put his feet up on the porch railing. "I am hungry again, though. Who does good delivery?" he called out over his shoulder.

"What?" My voice came out in a squeak.

Logan turned his head, and the grin was still in place. "Delivery. You know, food? I have to eat. I'll waste away otherwise. You don't want a dead body on your porch."

I leaned against the door frame again. Sweet baby Jee, this was getting worse and worse. First last night with Ash, and the police, and... I shuddered. There could be a dead body, if my worst fears about Ash were true. And I was the last person to see him. To hear Logan talking about a dead body so casually gave me the shivers.

Not to mention, him camped out on my porch was bound to cause questions.

Well, it would just have to cause questions. I closed the door with a bang, making sure to lock the deadbolt.

I heard Logan laugh. It was a rich, full laugh that echoed around my porch.

I didn't care. I marched upstairs, and got myself in the shower. Hopefully, he'd get the idea and leave. My indignation faded as I kept turning the water heat down.

I was just too darn hot. Not another hot flash. The water was nearly cold before I finished. I kept turning down the heat.

Once out of the shower, I got dressed, taking care to make sure my hair was decent, and dusted on some face powder, and then put on lip gloss. I couldn't explain why I was doing this, but it felt good. Actually, I was feeling pretty good today, at least physically, with the exception of my forearm. Well, and now that my brain fog had cleared. I'd been avoiding looking at it, but I did now. The tattoo was so real looking. I was caught by the detail, and the fact that the eyes looked as brilliant as they had when I'd tried on the bracelet.

How in the hell had the bracelet ended up on my arm as a tattoo?

Because you have been chosen, the light voice said.

"What?" I asked out loud.

You are chosen. This is only the beginning. Now you must prove yourself. If you fail, your life will never be the same.

"What? What does that mean?" I asked.

The path of discovery is yours to walk. Even as you have been chosen, you must demonstrate that you are ready. Don't take too long, the voice said.

"Who are you? Where are you?" I turned in a full circle, but it was only me in the bathroom, only me when I looked in the mirror.

A glint caught my eye, and I looked down. The tattoo, which was kind of glittery looking, almost looked like it was moving.

"What are you?" I whispered.

There was no reply.

I brushed my hair some more, not entirely happy with the look. Finally, I pulled it up into a loose bun, the one my daughter Rachel called 'the onion'. Basically, three wraps of a hair band, and poof the hair out, giving it a rounded shape. Today it did look like a lopsided onion.

Then I remembered. Logan had seen the tattoo, which meant I wasn't going crazy. He called it… I stopped, thinking. He'd called it the mark of the Oracle. The Oracle, with a capital 'O'.

Which meant he knew what this was.

I practically ran down the stairs and into the vestibule, yanking open the front door. Logan was still there, his feet still on my railing, looking like he had every right to be there, only now he was eating a huge sub sandwich.

"Sorry, I didn't order you one. I didn't know what you liked," he said, his mouth half full of food.

"Don't talk while you're eating," I said crossly.

He grinned, and chewed slowly, swallowed, and then said, "How can I help you?"

"I can't believe you ordered food."

"I get cranky if I get too hungry," he said. "And since I can't leave, I gotta eat."

"You do recognize this?" I stuck out my right arm, the serpent looking even more lively and glittery in the sunlight.

He nodded. "That's the mark of the Oracle."

I stared at him, not liking my options, but not seeing any other way. "Fine. You can come in. Close the door behind you and wipe your feet." I went back inside, hating that I had no choice. He wanted help, I wanted answers. Which meant I'd have to give a little to get a little. Hopefully not much more than a little.

I walked through the kitchen into the living room, and sat on the couch. "Sit," I said to Logan, pointing at the easy chair across from me.

He was almost too tall for the chair, but he folded himself into it. He began to speak before I could say anything else. "Wynter Chastain, Oracle of Theama—"

"What does that mean?" I asked in exasperation.

"What?" Logan looked confused.

"The Oracle of They—the—"

"Theh-eh-ma," Logan said slowly, sounding out for me. "That's what you are. The Oracle of Theama, the seer. You see things, the truth of things, for those who seek your help."

Another flash of light, and I fell forward, blinded as my forearm screamed in pain.

This was getting irritating.

When I opened my eyes, the first thing I noticed was that my tongue was stuck to the roof of my mouth.

"Gack," I said.

"Hey, hold on," a masculine voice said. A shadow moved through the room, and then Logan Gentry stood beside my bed, a glass of water in hand.

I took it, gulping down the water, trying to ease the dryness in my mouth. When I finished the glass, he took it, and filled it again from a pitcher next to the bed. "How are you feeling?"

"I don't even know," I said crossly. "Why are you still here? And how did I get here, in my bed? Why are you here?"

"Because you fell down in a faint in front of me again," he said, reminding me that I'd done the same thing last night. "I couldn't leave you lying on the floor," Logan continued reasonably. "I figured this would be the best place for you, since I didn't know how long you'd be out. Is fainting and passing out a habit for you? And are you at a place where you can talk without passing out?"

"Oh, sure," I said.

"Good," he said, either missing or ignoring my sarcasm. He pulled a chair—one of the dining room chairs, I noted—up close to the bed. "Is this the first time you've seen the mark of the Oracle?"

"You keep saying the Oracle like it's a thing," I said, my irritation growing. "Can we back up and have you tell me what the hell the Oracle is? I mean other than I'm supposed to tell you the truth. I can do that right now. You're a pushy jerk. There. The truth."

Logan stared at me. "You really don't know?"

"I don't know a damn thing," I said. "Which seems to be the way things are."

"What?" Logan looked confused.

"Nothing. What can you tell me?"

He gazed at me for a moment. "Can you remember how you got the tattoo?"

"I didn't even know it was there until you touched my arm," I said. "Was that last night? What time is it? What day is it?"

"It's about thirty minutes after you fell at my feet," Logan said, a small smile on his face.

I hated the way he said it, all smug-like. "That's it? I feel like I've been out drinking all night."

He shrugged. "I don't even pretend to know what the Oracle's deal is. I'm just telling you what I know."

"What is the Oracle?" I asked. I felt like I'd been asking this for ages. "Can you tell me that?"

"The Oracle of Theama is the person in the supernatural world—"

"Wait. Did you just say supernatural?" I asked.

His brows lowered. "Yes. Why?"

"Are you serious?" I asked.

"No. Why would I be joking? How do you think you got that tattoo?"

"A rogue tattoo artist?" I asked.

"No, that's not it. That's the mark of the Oracle," Logan said patiently.

I wished very much for my Taser. Very much. But something stopped me. This wasn't a guy who looked as though he were given to jokes, or pranks. He looked deadly serious and intense. And he knew about this thing on my arm. So maybe I'd have to keep my Taser inclinations under wraps for the time being. "And the Oracle?" I asked.

"Helps those in the supernatural world find answers," Logan replied promptly. "She is the one who can help to solve mysteries, find things that are lost, and bring the truth to light." He said this in a rush, like it was something he'd memorized.

I blinked, trying to take it all in. "You're telling me that's me?"

He nodded. "Only the Oracle has such a mark."

"Any tattoo artist could do this," I argued.

"No, they couldn't, Wynter."

The use of my name, said gently and with firm conviction, is what did me in. I leaned back against my headboard, letting the tears slide down my face. Normally, I hated people to see me cry. But I figured at this stage, I was beyond worrying about such things. "How did you find me?" I asked. I'd only met Ash last night. This armband, this bracelet—I'd slid it on last night, and fell forward into a blinding light then, too.

The bracelet that had disappeared, and hadn't been found, I realized.

"I did the Fire Ceremony," Logan said, handing me a tissue from the box on my nightstand, along with the glass of water again.

"The what?" I asked.

He rolled his eyes and shifted in his chair. "Come on, woman. The Fire Ceremony. It's a ritual to help those who are in need of the Oracle."

"Great! You mean anyone can find me?" I felt a surge of panic and hoped I wouldn't throw up. If I had to, however, I hoped it landed on Logan Gentry.

"No. When you do the ceremony, you have to genuinely be in need of help from the Oracle. If you're not, the location of the Oracle won't be revealed. It took me two weeks to get your location. I was getting worried that my quest wasn't worthy."

"You have to be worthy to get my help?" I asked, trying to get a handle on this.

"Yes. And if you aren't worthy, and you do the Fire Ceremony, you can get hurt. The magic involved can boomerang back to you in a major way. Not in a good major way, either."

"Well, you're obviously still whole," I said, looking him over. Which was a dangerous thing. Even as annoyed as I was, it didn't change the fact that Logan Gentry was one hell of a man wrapped in a very appealing package. He had a look of wildness around his edges. Probably why I'd been nervous. I could sense the wildness. It was almost animal in nature. The vision of his bare back, covered in small white scars, came back to me. Although I didn't think, well, not anymore at least, that he'd hurt me. He'd had plenty of time to do that, if harm was his goal. And according to him, he needed my help.

The problem was what would happen when I couldn't give it.

Logan nodded. "I know, thank the gods. I was getting concerned," he said, smiling.

The way his smile transformed his face nearly blew me away. Had I not been sitting in bed, I might have fallen down again. He was… gorgeous. Wow. "Okay, so you did the Fire Ceremony, and then?" I asked to cover my confusion and everything else.

"Well, like I said, I was getting desperate, and then the night before last, it showed me where to find you."

"How does it do that? A fire give directions, I mean?" I tried not to think about how completely bananas this sounded.

"It's like a vision. I guess…" he stopped for a moment, thinking. "It's like you get GPS coordinates, but in your head. And you know where to go."

"And only people with good intentions can get the coordinates?" I asked, feeling nervous.

"Yes. It's a way to protect the Oracle. There are always assholes who want to use others for their own gain. The Oracles have their own protection built in. I've also heard," Logan sat forward in his chair, "That if you try and harm an Oracle, you lose body parts, but you know how urban legends get started."

"I hope it's true," I said. "You know, if you have any nefarious ideas."

"You really have no idea about this?" He clasped his hands in front of him, and gazed at me, obviously ignoring my snide remark.

"No! I only found the..." what did I call the bracelet? "This mark on me last night. After I'd gone out to..." oh god. How to describe Ash? "Have drinks with a friend. We were at his place. I went into the bathroom, and when I came out, the room was trashed. I mean, I wasn't in there for long, but it was like someone turned the place upside down." I shivered, remembering.

"Go on," Logan said.

"And then I sat down, trying to figure out what to do, and I sat on something that poked me in the leg. I reached down into the chair, and pulled out a bracelet, an armband, really, that looked just like this," I rubbed my hand over my tattoo, which made a shiver run through my body. Okay. That was new. And discomforting.

"The Oracle chose you. That might be why it took me so long to find you. The old Oracle moved on. And you hadn't been chosen yet," Logan said, looking like he was working something out for himself.

"What does that mean?" I asked, running my hands through my hair.

"I don't know. Most of the knowledge of the Oracle is just what is needed for people to find her, and to keep her safe. The lore, or whatever? That is not something I'd know."

"How do I find out what the lore is?" I asked.

"I don't know."

"Okay, what is it you want me to find out for you?" I was trying to keep my temper from boiling over. He had information, but it wasn't enough. Damn it. It wasn't enough.

"I need you to help me find my past," Logan replied.

CHAPTER FIVE

*W*hatever I'd expected to hear from him, with regard to what he wanted, finding his past wasn't even anywhere near my bingo card. Logan and I talked for another hour, in which I determined that he didn't mean me harm. He answered my questions too patiently. I mean, it could all be a trap, but I didn't think so. I finally decided I'd have to trust him for the time being, and I got up and made an early dinner, deciding that I would invite him to join me. I wasn't happy with him, or the things he was telling me, but something in the way he'd told me what he was looking for made me… god in hell… want to help him. Was this part of being the Oracle?

"You can stay for dinner, if you like," I said. "But you need to either help, or sit down and stop looming." I figured I owed it to him. I'd passed out in front of him… what? Three times? And he hadn't left me to die a lonely death any of those times, even as my memory was kind of touch and go for a bit.

He'd sat down, which I was glad about. I didn't really want the help.

My back was to Logan, who'd taken a seat at the kitchen island.

"You have no magic, no witches, or anything like that in your family?" Logan asked me.

"No," I said, without turning around. "Cheating lying husband who passed away, but no witches."

"I'm sorry," Logan said, his words sincere.

"So am I," I said. "What are you? A witch? A wizard? What?"

He was silent for a moment, and then said, "A shifter."

I turned to look at him then, spoon still in my hand. "You're kidding me. Shifters are real?"

Logan didn't reply, only nodded.

"Is it all right to ask what kind of shifter you are?" I had no idea of the etiquette of all this. I didn't want to say the wrong thing. The other part of me thought I should be calling the cops and getting this madman out of my house, but... I couldn't. There was something about him that rang true.

"I'm a panther," he said.

"You're a..." my voice trailed off as I looked at him. "I can see that," I said finally.

He smiled, and I saw the animal edge. That's why it was there. Because he had an animal side.

Well. This was interesting.

"What is it about your past that's lost?"

Logan sighed. "I don't have a past beyond seven years ago."

I turned around again. "What?"

"Don't burn whatever it is you're making," he said, smiling. "It smells good, and I've been eating a lot of take-out food the past week."

"Oh, we're past the stage of concern. It's all over but the cooking," I said, waving a hand at the stove. The beef stroganoff was one of my family favorites, a go-to after we'd all be running around all day at swim practice, or soccer practice, or band, or all three. Easy, and finished by the time the kids finished their homework. "Talk."

"Now you're interested?" He leaned back in the chair he sat in.

"Who wouldn't be? I have no idea if I can help you, so you might as well tell me. If I can't, it's a good story for book club."

He nodded. "I woke up in the middle of the Mojave Desert. I was wearing jeans that were ripped to hell, and I eventually found a light yellow tee shirt nearby, also torn to shreds, near me. I was covered in blood. You saw my back earlier?" Logan asked.

I nodded, feeling a little queasy at the memory of all the small white scars all over his back.

"Well, they were all cut up and bleeding, and covered in sand and bugs, and gods knows what else. I lay there in the sun, the shredded shirt over my eyes, wanting to die, and then I sat up and thought, to hell with this. I didn't want to die." He sighed, looking out the far window into the night. "Six nights later, I shifted. I had no idea what was happening, no idea about anything. Kind of like you feel now, but worse. No money, no home, no shoes, no name," Logan finished. "I chose my name, after I got help from another shifter who found me." His eyes closed briefly, and I saw the spasm of pain that moved across his angular features. "But no matter what, I can't remember anything beyond waking up in that gods forsaken desert and wanting to die. I always knew I had to find out, but I've never felt like it was the right time. About a month ago, something changed. I went to an apothecary and asked for an Oracle bundle—"

I held up a hand. "What is an Oracle bundle?"

"It's a special bunch of herbs that allows you to ask for help from the oracle. Only apothecaries sell it." He shrugged. "Sure, there's black market stuff, but remember, you can't get help from the Oracle if your intentions are not sincere. So there's really no need for a black market. Anyway, I got the bundle, and I researched how to do the Fire Ceremony, and that's when I started looking for you."

"Where did you find out how to do the ceremony?" I asked.

"Online. Where you find everything," Logan grinned.

Talk turned to my kids then, Logan having seen a picture of them on the fridge. I learned that he and his friend Mark, the shifter who had found and helped him, thought that he was in his mid to late forties. Truthfully, even though he looked like a man who spent time outside, he didn't look a day over thirty, or thirty-five. He had no family that he knew of. "No one came looking for me," he said, with dark humor. I heard the pain in those words.

Once dinner was ready, we sat at the island.

"This is good. Thank you for cooking for me, and not pepper spraying me again. This is delicious," Logan said. As if to emphasize his point, he took a large bite of the stroganoff.

"You're lucky I didn't have my Taser," I said.

"You carry a Taser?"

"My late husband traveled a lot. I carry a number of things."

He laughed, a loud, roaring laugh. "You're a surprise, Wynter."

"It sounds like that's going to be a good thing for me," I said.

"Probably. But you have to know this. The Oracle is important. I'm going to guess and say the Oracle armband, or bracelet, chooses the next oracle, and you've been chosen. There are things in place, things I probably have no idea about, that will help to keep you safe."

"It would be great if I could figure out what those things were, or where I might find them," I said. "So what's the deal? I have to help everyone who comes to me? Why me? Why not a private investigator?"

"You're the original investigator," Logan said. "Maybe not you, but the role you're in."

"I didn't choose this. And obviously people are looking for… for this," I gestured at the armband-slash-tattoo. "Or at least, the person who has this. What if I don't want to help someone? Do I have to anyway?"

"Well, it's kind of like everyone has to pass a test before they even get to you," he said. "You're not going to end up with shady people, generally. I think that the answer to that is yes, though. You're obligated to help."

"I didn't sign up for this," I said, and I was angry to find that I could feel tears hovering at the edge of my eyes.

"You did. It's the oath you took," Logan said.

"I didn't take an oath, I didn't swear one damned thing, not to anyone," I said angrily, putting down my fork.

"Yes, you did," Logan insisted.

"How the hell do you know that?" I asked.

He reached over, and his large hand grabbed my forearm, holding it up with his hand just below the tattoo.

"This. This is your oath. It's your job now, your calling. It's your responsibility to do it to the best of your ability."

"I don't want this," I said softly. "How do I get it off?"

He let go of my arm. "You don't. It's until death do you part, sister."

I looked at him, my eyes getting wider and wider. "Please go," I whispered. Then I burst into tears, and ran from the room. I raced up to the bedroom, slamming the door behind me.

I didn't want this. I didn't ask for it. And now I had to worry about every magical Tom, Dick and Scary Harry from the world of things that went bump in the night showing up at my house, wanting a favor.

There had to be a way out of this. I got into bed again, and cried myself to sleep.

That night, I dreamed again. It didn't start out with the book floating in front of me, drawing me in. No, tonight started out very differently.

I kept seeing the tall brunette beauty of Natalie, the other Mrs. Chastain. I could see her with Derek, both of them tall and attractive. It was disturbing, and I found myself tossing and turning in bed. I didn't want to see her, or them together. I didn't want to see them with their kids, looking for all the world like the picture perfect family. No. Stop it, I thought. Go away.

The space in front me shifted, almost like someone had waved their hands and a curtain had been drawn, or pulled. I was in a room, a room I didn't recognize, but that didn't feel completely unfamiliar, either. This time, the book was further away from me than it had been in my earlier dream. I looked around, and the room was small, cramped. There were a lot of books, all older looking, and the place looked like it smelled musty. Forgotten. The book was on a table in the middle of the room, and there were tables that lined the walls, thinner, more like workbenches, with shelves over them. Bottles, also old looking, and bunches of flowers and weeds lined the tables. Papers, quills, pens and pencils were littered among the bottles and books.

It was a mess.

The book in the center of the room, the one I'd dreamed about before, still sparkled and glowed, but this time, as I went to walk closer to it, the room shifted, and a door slammed in my face.

"No!" I cried out. I needed to see the room, the book. I threw myself against the door, my fingers scrabbling at the wood. "No, please, no!" The door flew open once more. This time, I was back in the room with the glowing, sparkling book, and the shelves and workbenches loaded with crap, but I was able to look around, and able to resist the urge to grab the book from where it sat on the little table in the middle of this weird room. There was a door, tall, wooden, painted black, and tonight, I walked to the door, and opened it. The room outside of my dream room was blurry, not in focus. My sense was of a room with a lot of things in it. Cluttered was the word that came to mind. But I couldn't seem to focus on any one thing in particular, any one thing that would give me an idea of where this was.

When I woke up, I could feel the dried tracks of tears on my face. I touched them, feeling the stiffness of the dried salt. Was this from crying in my dream?

What in the world was going on? I'd thought the week of learning Derek had died was the worst of my life. Then it was last week, when I found out about Natalie. But the last two days were quickly taking the top spot as the most upsetting of my life. There were things happening that were completely out of my control, and there was seemingly nothing I could do.

I got out of bed, searching in my nightstand until I found a pen and notebook. I took the time to write down everything I remembered from the dream. I had no idea if this would help, but isn't this what Oracles did? I mean, if Logan was telling me the truth.

Logan. Oh, lord. What had happened to him? I'd run off after telling him to leave, and I had no idea if he was still lurking around. Although maybe I could ease up on calling him a lurker. I'd pepper sprayed him, and he hadn't called the police. Given my recent run in with them, I had to admit I was glad. Then he'd helped me when I kept passing out.

So maybe he wasn't a creepy lurker.

It was just too much, too much to take in. All of this—Ash, the bracelet, the multiple faints, and learning that not only was there magic and shifters—had happened within two days.

The weight of my thoughts made me tired. I put the notebook back on my nightstand and crawled back into bed. It was still dark. Maybe I could get a little more sleep.

The next morning, I took my time getting ready. I wasn't sure that I wanted to go downstairs and see what awaited me. But when I came down into the kitchen, I found the kitchen clean and tidy, and a fresh pot of coffee hot and waiting. A note sat on the counter.

Winter, it said, spelling my name wrong. I'd have to tell him the right way to spell it. I continued reading.

I stayed the night. I didn't want to leave when you were upset. Thanks for dinner and the comfortable couch. I got word that one of my clients has a job for me. I'll be back in two days. I'm sorry I couldn't give you more info, but I'll see what I can find out while I'm gone.

Logan

All that day, I went about my chores—laundry, because good god, my laundry pile was getting ridiculous, cleaning out the fridge, vacuuming, and generally putting the house in order. I tried not to think about all that I'd learned in the past forty-eight hours. I rubbed at the tattoo, but it didn't tell me anything.

Tell me anything. The words caught in my brain. When I'd met Logan, something—a distinct voice, one that sounded male, but like from far away, like someone was speaking in a tunnel—told me he wasn't an enemy.

Who had that been?

Was I slowly and decisively losing my mind?

When I went to bed, worn out from all the house chores, I fell right asleep. I'd tried to take a hot shower before bed since it usually helped me sleep, but I'd had to make the shower cold again, because I was definitely feeling overheated. What I really wanted was to dream tonight. To find out more about the room. The book.

Sure enough, I was back in the room, and I turned to walk out the door, barely sparing a glance for the items in the room that had once fascinated me, although I gazed longingly at the book. *Not long now,* I thought.

Where had that come from?

While I was thinking about it, I walked out the door, and into the cluttered room that I couldn't see clearly. Tonight, I saw more. It was like things were piled on top of each other, and like the room with the book, I got the sense of musty and old. But I kept walking, not stopping to look at anything in particular. I came to a stairway, and stopped.

Did I need to go up? Before I even finished the thought, I was headed up the stairs, and out through another room, brighter than the one downstairs, but still fuzzy and lacking in clarity. I walked toward the door with the brightest shaft of sunlight and went through it.

I was outside. I turned around in a three hundred and sixty degree circle, wanting to see where I was. Then I saw it. I looked around, to the left and the right of the building. I knew where this was, where the door that led to the book was. I knew exactly where I needed to go.

When I got up the next morning, I showered and was out the door shortly after the sun rose fully in the sky. I knew what I'd seen in my dream. A small shop, with a dusty and crooked sign that said Community Meeting Place. I'd seen it before, years ago. It was an abandoned looking building in Danvers, about three hours away. If you weren't from Massachusetts, you wouldn't know that Danvers is the original Salem. In Danvers, the Community Meeting Place was between a flower shop and the High Street Cemetery. My kids used to love to tour Danvers, and then go to the more commercial Salem when they were younger. I knew the area well. I checked the ferry schedule, and drove like a bat out of hell to the ferry depot, just making the ferry that would take me across Vineyard Sound to Woods Hole. It was a long drive from there, but I knew that I needed to do this.

I sang as I drove along, feeling like even though I was heading out on no more than a hunch, and that wasn't very wise. But what else did I have to do? I called each of the kids while I drove, telling them I was doing some decluttering, and cleaning out of the house. I didn't want them to worry, or worse, want to come home and see me. Not with this armband tattoo, and a man who said he was a panther, and the Oracle, and the dreams. No. I needed to make sure they didn't feel they needed to be with me.

"You're up early, Mom," Rachel said, a thread of worry in her tone.

"I know. I went to bed early last night and got a full night's sleep," I said, lying through my teeth.

"How are you doing?" she asked.

"I'm still mad. I'll probably be mad for a while," I said. "But I've settled the claim, and the money's there for when you all need it."

"We've been talking about that, Mom," Rachel said.

"No," I said. "The house is paid off, I sold the company, and invested that in my retirement. This is for you. This is what we planned." I didn't tell her that I'd have to budget. That was for me to worry about. Not her, not any of my kids.

"Well, everything's changed now," Rachel said, and I could tell she was about to cry. "So we need to change as well, Mom."

"Have all three of you decided this?" I asked.

"We have."

"I'm not agreeing," I said.

"Oh, of course not. Why in the world would you do that?" Rachel was impatient now, tears no longer in evidence.

"But I'm willing to talk with you. How about you come by this weekend, all three of you? Saturday afternoon, and we'll talk."

"Okay," Rachel said, and I could tell that this was more than she'd expected. "There's something else, Mom," she said.

"Nathan and Sophie," I said immediately. The names of her half siblings. Of Derek's children with another woman.

"You said you didn't think the other woman—"

"Natalie," I said.

"Natalie, right. You said you didn't think she knew."

"I still think that," I said. My social media stalking told me that.

"Well, I think we should get in touch with her. Maybe just us, if you don't want to," Rachel said.

"Worried I'll cause a scene?" I asked, not completely amused.

"Mom, I keep thinking about what if this was me, what would I do, and I fall right into crazy town. I'd be so angry. I want to kill Dad, and I wasn't married to him."

My anger disappeared instantly. "Oh, honey, if he lied to us both, how can I blame her?"

"How can you not?" Rachel shot back.

"Well, I did, for about a week. Thought a lot of snide thoughts about her tall, tan self."

"You've met her?" Rachel practically yelled.

"No. I have looked at her social media," I admitted. "You were with me," I added. I was *not* going to admit just how much I'd looked. Some things you needed to keep to yourself.

"Well, I'd be doing the same. Probably stalker level," Rachel said. "Totally understandable. I'll be honest, I was only focused on the two little kids."

I wondered how she'd missed the tall, beautiful woman standing next to her dad, but I kept that to myself.

"Why do you want to get in touch with the kids?" I asked. I wasn't upset, I didn't think. At least not right now. But I was curious.

"Because he was their dad, too. And while he's a complete schmuck, and a jerk and a lying cheater, I loved him. I miss him," her voice got small. "I bet they do, too."

"Honey, you're such a good person," I said, feeling a lump in my throat. "We'll definitely talk about how to move forward with your brother and sister." It was like acid in my throat to call them that, to acknowledge once and for all my husband had another family—but what was more important? Being right, or doing the best for my kids?

I'd take the latter every single time.

Rachel and I hung up after a round of *I love you's*, and I continued on toward Danvers, feeling even better than I had before. So what if a large portion of my life was unknown? I'd figure it out. For the first time, I honestly felt that. I'd Googled the Community Meeting Place, and it hadn't shown up on the map. But the cemetery and the flower shop were still there, and when I looked at the street photos, there was a building with faded lettering on a sign that looked like what I'd seen in my dream. I was on the right track. I knew it. I could feel it.

The only question was, what would I find when I got there?

CHAPTER SIX

The weird little building was still there, between the cemetery and the florist, although the florist shop looked different than what I remembered. No matter. I parked my car, and got out.

God, this place looked abandoned. There were only a few cars in the parking lot, most of them older models. There was a navy blue van parked next to the cemetery entrance. It had chrome bumpers and there was a dent on the rear fender breaking the smooth silver of the chrome. I watched it for a couple of minutes, delaying, trying to work up the courage to walk in to the Community Meeting Place building. Then I took a deep breath, got out of my car, and went straight for the front door.

When I pulled it open, a bell tinkled to announce my arrival. I took two steps in and stopped.

The Community Meeting Place looked like the worst junk shop I'd ever been in. There were piles of old furniture, trunks, cabinets, books stacked on every surface. There were small walkways that allowed you to move through the piles of stuff, but they were narrow. Holy Joseph. I hugged my purse to me, not wanting to touch anything. If something began to fall, I might get buried in this and never be found.

After scooching my way through, I reached the back of the building, and found that there was a counter. Amazingly, a man stood behind the counter, glaring at me. "Can I help you?" he asked in the tone of one who is deeply offended.

"Well, I was—"

"There's not a lot left," he said, waving a hand around.

I couldn't even respond. There wasn't a lot left? How full had this building been?

"Most of the local covens and mages have picked the place over, but you're welcome to look around. If you find something, come back and ring the bell." He stopped, and glared even more intensely. "If you try to leave without telling me, I'll know."

"Okay, but what—"

"I need to go and feed Mr. Platypus. He's my cat, and he doesn't like his lunch to be late," the man said, and walked away. "Don't try and sneak away!" he called over his shoulder as he disappeared into a door at the end of the counter.

"This is so strange," I said out loud. "Why did he run away? Why do I need to check in before leaving?" But I'd seen the door in my dream, and when I walked out, it was this building. Although my dream hadn't shown the enormity of all the junk in here. I might have just driven over three hours for nothing, but I had to check.

"Well, let's go take a look," I said out loud, and started to wander around the pathways, peering through what I could.

There was another room to the right of the counter, and while not only was it darker and far less inviting, I walked into the room. I had to check everywhere. This was the place in my dream, and since I'd been dreaming of the book, the room, and now the Community Meeting Place any time I closed my eyes in the last two days, I couldn't leave until I'd gone over everything. Although I wasn't sure how I was supposed to check at the bottom of the various piles.

The darker side room wasn't as crowded, and I could see now what the man meant when he said things were picked over. Drawers on desks and in cabinets were pulled out, there were papers strewn about, and it was obvious that people had been going through the furniture in here. But no one put anything back—it was like they found what they wanted, and just left.

This was no way to run a shop. Even one as weird as this.

I saw a dim light shining at the back of the room, and I walked toward it. The light lit a tiny, narrow stairway. "How many rooms does this have?" I asked to no one in particular. I couldn't tell if this was the stairway in my dream. In the dream, I'd walked upstairs, not gone down them.

Keep looking, I heard someone say.

"What?" I turned around and around. I'd heard this voice before—but where? It was like a dream where you remember small bits of it during the next day, but you can't ever get a grip on the details of the dream. The voice was light, but firm.

I didn't hear the voice again, but I still kept looking. Walking forward, I kept looking to see if anything from the dreams I'd been having that I did remember were in this room.

Nothing.

I walked into the next room, and sneezed as what felt like a wall of dust hit me. Wiping at my eyes, I peered into the gloom. I couldn't see the far wall, so maybe I was coming to the end of the rabbit warrens of rooms in this place. I walked further in. It got darker.

Pulling out my phone, I turned on the flashlight, and scanned the room. Something over in the corner caught my eye, and I panned the light back to the far corner.

A door.

I stopped, the phone dropping down in my hand and almost to the floor as I tried to process what I was seeing. It was the door, the door I'd seen in my dreams. I caught the phone, and shone the light toward the wall.

Holy crow. It was the door I'd seen in my dreams. Even though I knew I had to drive up here, had to see—I didn't expect to actually *see* the door. But there it was. Real, right across the room from me.

I make my way across the room, and stop in front of the door. Dark, maybe blue, or black, dusty, with a worn brass door knob. This is the door. This was real.

My armband-slash-tattoo. The dreams. The shifter named Logan. The Oracle.

It was all real.

Taking a breath, I put my hand on the doorknob. As soon as my hand touched the doorknob, the door vanished.

"What in the world?" I ask out loud. There's no more door, just a wall with wood paneling on the upper half of the wall, and red bricks below the paneling.

"Would you hurry up?" a voice asked in my ear. This was a woman, and she sounded quite put out.

This was different from the voice that told me to keep looking. What was going on? Was I going mad? Hearing two voices in the same day? This voice was definitely a woman, and an older woman. She reminded me of my grandmother. Terse and impatient. If I went to a doctor with these complaints, they'd toss me in a hospital and throw away the key.

"I can't find the door," I said out loud. What now?

Which made me equally sort of bonkers, but there was no one here. Except the unfriendly guy at the counter, and according to him, he was attending to Mr. Platypus the cat.

"I haven't got all day," the older woman's voice said. It sounded like she was right next to me. "I'm already through a pack, waiting on you."

"That makes two of us," I snapped. "I haven't got all day, either."

I did not imagine the cackle in my ear.

"Who are you?" I asked out loud.

"Someone who doesn't have all day," the woman said again. "So get a move on."

I turned around slowly, letting my flashlight shine onto what looked like never ending piles of clutter. There was no one else down here with me. I pointed my phone's flashlight along the wall. "There's nothing there," I said.

The woman didn't have anything to say at that point. Figures. No, the only voices I heard were those that made my life more difficult, but did nothing to help me. I wasn't giving up, however. Not when I'd come all this way.

Stepping closer, I ran my hand along the wall. My hand caught and as quickly as the door had disappeared before, it was there. What was this? I put my hand on the door knob and the door swung open.

Just as it was when I saw the door, this room was straight out of my dreams. The workbenches along the wall, the table in the middle of the room, and on the table sat the book. The thing that had started all my dreams. I walked into the room, unable to stay away from the book, which almost looked like it was emitting sparks. As I got close, I stretched out my hand, laying it right in the middle of the cover.

And everything went black.

Okay, this whole passing out, blinding white light, things going pitch black—it was getting old. "I'm tired of this!" I shouted. "Just show me what's going on!" I opened my eyes. I was sitting on the front porch of a small wooden house. Wherever I was, I wasn't in Danvers anymore.

I sat in a chair that was covered in yellow flowered plastic.

Across from me was an older woman, her hair fluffed out around her in a white halo that was brighter in the sunlight.

"Who are you?" I asked.

The woman eyed me. She had a can of Olympia beer in one hand, and a cigarette in the other, the smoke from the cigarette rising and curling up into her hair.

She wore a floral print nightdress, and over the night-dress, a light pink housecoat. One foot was propped on her other knee, spotlighting her blue fluffy slippers. "Name's Florry. Thought you'd never get here." Her slippered foot jiggled a little. The slippers had seen better days.

"Where is here? You were expecting me?" I could barely get the words out. "Who are you? What is this all about? Why am I seeing this book and this room in my dreams to the point that I had to drive half way across the state to come here? How did I get from the room with the book to wherever here is? And what in the name of all that is holy is this?" I held out my arm where the serpent armband tattoo was bright, even in the dim light of this room.

"Whoa, whoa, sister. Calm down. I can help you, for sure. I can even answer some of your questions. But you gotta relax." She leans back in her chair, and takes a pull off her cigarette.

"And how did I get here?" I asked. There is so much I wanted—needed—to ask. This is crazy, but I've hit the point where I'm desperate to know answers. "How can I relax? My whole life is upside down, my husband—" I stopped in horror as the tears filled my eyes, almost as though they'd been waiting for the right moment.

"What about your husband?" Florry asked in a different tone.

I managed to get out what happened, with the recent revelations, in between crying that became outright sobbing. When my sobbing calmed to hiccups, Florry got up and went inside. She came back out with a glass of water and a box of tissues.

I took it gratefully, and gulped it down. I thought I moved past the sobbing about Derek stage. I guess I hadn't yet. Once I finished the water I set the glass down. "How is this possible? Am I really here?"

Florry lit a fresh cigarette, looking out across the field in front of her house. "'Here' is a relative term, toots. You're here with me, sure. And you drank the water. But as to where you really are... it's kind of a limbo question."

"What does that mean?" I asked. "I appreciate you listening, because obviously I needed to get that out, but—"

"That's why it's all happening now," Florry said. She looked directly at me. "If your husband was still here, you would have never found the armband." She eyed me. "How old are you?"

"Well, of course I wouldn't have found the bracelet!" I sat up straight. "I would have never gone out to a bar."

Florry shook her head. "It's more than that," she said. "I don't know this for sure, but after being the Oracle for thirty-plus years—"

I held up a hand. "Wait a minute. You were the Oracle for over thirty years?"

She nodded. "Thirty-three, if you're looking for accuracy. At least, I'm pretty sure that's how long it was. Anyway, I found the armband in that field right over there," she pointed across the road with her cigarette. "My kids were grown, and my husband had been gone for about a year."

"I'm so sorry," I said. Did the Oracle only prey on widows?

She snorted. "I'm not. Gerald was a right piece of trash, and he finally left with some woman who sadly fell for his nonsense. Never saw 'em again, and good riddance."

"Why—" I started.

Florry waved a hand. "People my age don't leave. Not here. But we're not talking about me. We're talking about being the Oracle. Since you're sporting Goldie on your arm, I'm guessing you have your first consultant?"

"My first what? Who's Goldie?"

"You turned around one day and some supe was lounging around your house," Florry said abruptly.

That was so accurate I laughed. "Yes. He wouldn't leave."

She snorted, leaning back. "They never do."

We both laughed then.

Florry sat up, and stared at me directly. "To be fair, they can't leave. If they found you, it's because their cause is determined to be worthy."

"Worthy by who?" I interrupted.

"The universe. My old aunt Myrtle. Who knows?" Florry shot back. "In order for someone to seek out the Oracle, they have to do the Fire Ceremony—"

"Logan mentioned that," I said, pleased to actually understand something.

She nodded. "And if their cause is considered true and worthy, the location of the Oracle is revealed to them."

"How?"

"I think it's latitude and longitude coordinates. I've never done the ceremony, so I don't know. It could be different for everyone. It doesn't matter," Florry puffed on her cigarette. "The important thing for you to know is that they have already been judged, vetted if you will. The Oracle is never revealed to those of dark purpose, or dark hearts, or those seeking to do harm." She closed her eyes. "It's the only way we're protected."

"That's it? I have to help all those who show up at my door?"

She nodded, her eyes still closed. "If you don't, you'll get sick as a dog. You never had a hangover that feels as bad as what happens if you try to turn a consultant away."

"You know this from experience?" I asked.

Her eyes opened. "'Course I do. Everyone gets a wild hair at some point, gets tired of having their lives managed by a damn bracelet." Her gaze was fierce, then it softened. "Can I see it?"

"What?"

"The serpent," Florry said.

I held out my right arm.

"He's as beautiful as he ever was," she said quietly. "Has he spoken to you yet? Goldie? Have you heard him?"

"It talks?"

She nodded.

"It's a he?"

Florry shrugged. "It always sounded like a young man's voice to me. Very light, almost like listening to choir boys singing in church."

"That's very poetic," I said.

"Have you heard him?"

"Does he issue warnings?" I asked, thinking about the voice I'd been hearing.

"He's very cryptic at the beginning, and that doesn't get much better," Florry admitted. "But he is helpful at times."

"Is Goldie his name?"

She shook her head then, her curls waving around her face. "No. I don't know what his name is. I always called him Goldie, because he glitters so," she pointed at my arm. "The shimmer never goes away." Her voice was wistful.

She missed him, I realized.

"The details," I said, looking at the scales. My finger came up to stroke it. "This is real, isn't it? It's really happening? Why me?"

Florry didn't respond right away. She smoked her cigarette, the smoke curling above her head. The whole area was quiet, only the slight breeze stirring anything around us. "You said you knew where the Community Meeting Place was? When you saw it in your dreams?"

I nodded. "Yes. When my dream finally took me outside the building where the door to the book room was, I knew exactly where it was. I'd seen it years before."

"You're magic," she said.

"No," I replied instantly.

"Yes," she nodded. "Only those with magic can see that place. It's a beacon for those of us in the magical world, a place that we can go, be safe. Usually, find what you're looking for. It's why you're there now," Florry said, grinning. The grin transformed her entire face, and I could see what she looked like when she was younger. "It was time for you to finally go inside."

"How is that possible?" I asked.

Florry shrugged. "Who knows? After all these years, there are some things you'll never know. But you'll learn a lot, my girl. And you're ready for it."

"I don't know about that," I said.

"I do. The Oracle chooses carefully. There's only one thing."

"Which is?" I asked.

"Has Goldie warned you? Said you have to help this guy who showed up on your porch?"

"Something like that," I said.

"Well, he's right. You have to prove yourself, prove that you're capable of handling the job."

"What does that mean?"

"Find the answer to whatever your consultant is asking."

"How?" I threw up my hands. "I have no idea how to find his past."

"Pay attention to your dreams. And anything odd that happens." She nodded, like that answered all the questions.

"That really doesn't help," I said, putting the empty glass down on a small wicker table next to the chair where I sat.

"It brought you to the Community Meeting Place, and the grimoire," Florry said. "You can also look in the grimoire for help in dealing with situations. It's never going to give you a straight answer. You need to know that right off the bat. It will show you what you need to know, only when you need to know it. And even that won't give you straight answers. That's not how things work. You must find your own way," she said softly. She looked at me. "We all have to. Find our own way, I mean. Every Oracle is different." She nodded, and leaned back in her chair, lighting another cigarette.

I couldn't speak. There was so much information.

"Oracles are fluid," Florry said, looking out across the field. "We can offer answers. But those answers can change because people change. You need to tell anyone who comes looking for help that, too," she said. "Make it clear. They'll cry and moan and carry on later when things aren't exactly as they seem, but as long as you tell them that their actions, the actions of those around them, life in general, can change their future, and thus, the answers they seek, you're covered. What's important is that they know nothing is for sure. If they don't like it, too bad. We don't give absolutes." She shrugged and took another puff on her cigarette.

"Oh, no," I said. I hadn't said anything of the sort to Logan. What would that mean for him? For me? Worrying about our collective safety brought another thought to mind. "What about the man who had the bracelet?"

"Say what?" Florry looked interested.

I told her about Ashton Flint, and the night I found the bracelet.

She snorted again. "Goldie does like to make an entrance. You could make it easier, you old bat!" She addressed my arm. "But he won't," she said to me. "It's not his way. I'm sure Flint is fine. He was the vehicle to get the bracelet to you."

"Where is the bracelet now?"

"It's on your arm, part of you. That's why it sparkles like it does."

I looked down at the serpent coiled on my forearm. "I thought it was a tattoo."

"Nope. That's Goldie, and he'll be with you until you die, unless you fail with your first consultant."

"What happens if I fail?" I ask.

"I've always heard loss of memory, every piece of bad luck possible, and death. Since I don't know of any Oracles that failed, it could be all just a bunch of rubbish."

"There are more of us? Will I be able to talk to them, too?"

"No. You can access the wisdom of the former Oracles via the grimoire, and you have me, but you won't see the former Oracles."

"What are you, the Welcome Wagon?" I asked.

"Exactly that," Florry grinned. "But I kind of like the peace of being dead, so don't get all crazy and be calling on me at all times. I'll be around." She stood up, and came over to pick up the water glass. "You need to get back now. It's not good for the living to spend so much time in between."

"In between what?" I asked, standing up.

"Between life and death," Florry said as she opened up her screen door. "Go on home, and read the grimoire, whatever it shows you, and see what you can do for your consultant. It won't answer all your questions, but it will put you on the right path. I'll be seeing you." She walked inside the small house, the screen door slamming behind her.

"Wait!" I shouted, reaching for the screen door. "How do I—"

"I'm not a map. You'll find your way. All the Oracles do," came from inside the house. "Now go back, Wynter!"

I blinked at her harsh tone, and then I was back in the small dusty room, my hands on the book, the grimoire, Florry had called it, and the light from my phone making the one bright spot in the otherwise dark room. The book looked like it was emitting little sparks, just like in my dreams. My head was spinning, and I leaned against the book, my head touching the leather.

The book was humming.

I was too—tired? Exhausted? Confused? To do anything more than just stand there, and let things stop whirling around me.

When I was able to stand, I picked up the grimoire. It was heavy, but the weight felt right in my hand. I cradled it in the crook of my left arm.

It's time to go, I heard in my head.

"Goldie?" I asked.

There was silence, and then a noise that sounded like a huff. *You've met Florry.*

"Yes. Are you Goldie?"

I suppose, said the voice.

Now that I listened, I heard what Florry meant about choir boys in church. Light and high, although I might argue that Goldie could be female as well. But that didn't seem to matter, so I wasn't going to make a thing of it.

"Why haven't you told me more?" I demanded.

Part of accepting the Oracle is finding your own way there, Goldie said.

I rolled my eyes, even though Goldie couldn't see me. Or maybe he could. I looked down at my forearm. "Great. So I have a book, a ghost, and a bracelet that will kind of give me answers. But not really, because I have to find my own way. I guess I'm all set."

You are, said Goldie. *You have many assets at your disposal. But we need to leave now. You have found what you needed.*

"Keep your hair on," I muttered, walking from the room with the grimoire still cradled in my arm. I didn't want to let go go it, although it was heavy. Once I crossed the threshold of the door, I heard a bang. When I turned around, there was no door. The wall was solid as though there had never been a door.

I made my way back up the stairs, and then toward the counter at the back of the building. After the dim light downstairs, it seemed overly bright up here.

"Hello?" I called out. "I found something. I need to—"

"Then you need to leave," the man I'd initially seen came charging out of somewhere in the back. He gave a once over, stopping when he saw the book in the crook of my arm. "Once you have what you need, it's time for you to leave. Good bye." He nodded as though it were all settled, and marched back through the door he'd come out of.

I blinked, not sure what to do. But he told me to leave, and Florry told me that people only came here to find what they needed. I guess payment wasn't part of that. So I left. I walked out slowly, hoping I didn't set off any alarms, or anything like that. The Community Meeting Place didn't seem the sort of shop to have them, but you never knew.

No one came charging after me, no alarms went off, and I got to my car with no problems. The same three old cars and blue van were still there, but just as when I arrived, there were no other people around. The parking lot was quiet as I drove away.

I kept a hand on the grimoire all the way home.

CHAPTER SEVEN

 hen I pulled up into my driveway, the house was dark, outside of the hall light I could see from here. I walked carefully up to the porch, but Logan wasn't around. I couldn't tell if I was glad or disappointed that he wasn't here. His note had said he'd be gone for two days, so I had the rest of tonight and another full day to get a grip on what was happening to me.

The grimoire was cradled in my arm again, and I could feel it humming. I got inside, locking the doors carefully behind me. Then I went around and made sure all the doors were locked. I don't know why, but I felt... protective. Like I wanted to make sure that no one could get in.

Which made me feel paranoid, and I definitely didn't care for the feeling.

I made myself a sandwich, and poured out a glass of wine. The grimoire sat on the table next to me, near my laptop. I opened up the laptop, and started looking up Oracles.

The most famous one was in Greece, called the Oracle of Delphi. One article I read said that it was the one place where women ruled. Everything else at the time was centered around men. The people who came looking for answers were called consultants. Which was weird. Consultant meant expert of some sort. But these people were looking for help. I shook my head. It didn't matter. Now, I knew where Florry got the word.

Okay. I kept reading. Lots of discussion about how the Oracle tended to speak in rhymes, allowing for inter-pretation of their prophecies. The Oracle of Delphi was centered around a fissure that sent out smelly fumes, where a baby god Apollo had slain a Pythia serpent. I touched Goldie on my arm. The serpent. To find the answers of the consultants, the Oracle herself would breathe in the fumes before she gave answers.

Well, at least I didn't have to breathe in stinky gases that were probably poison. That was a plus. I continued reading.

The Oracles were all women. First, they were young and virginal, but the men seeking answers wouldn't always treat these young women appropriately. So gradually, the Oracles became older women, who gave up their entire lives and identities, and became the Oracle. That went along with Florry's comment about only women who had no ties to hold them back in daily life being chosen.

This whole thing had a root in mythology. Gazing down at Goldie, I wondered how much of it was true. More than I would have ever thought a week ago. Logan hadn't called me the Oracle of Delphi, however. He'd called me the Oracle of Theama. This was real. It wasn't going away. My fingers ran over Goldie's scales, slightly raised on my skin, like a real tattoo.

I closed out all my windows, tired of focusing on this particular problem and logged into my social media, going directly to Natalie Chastain's page. Time for a different problem. The thought made me smile, although without a lot of humor.

She'd taken down the recent pictures of Derek. I could tell that some of the pictures that had been there before, ones with the kids that I'd stared at through a haze of tears, had been removed. I scrolled through her feed to be sure. Yep. They were gone. None of her with him and the kids. Just her and the kids. One from yesterday. I peered at her. Her eyes were sad, and the happiness that I'd seen when I first looked her up, the smile that lifted her eyes—it was gone.

She knew. If I wasn't sure before, I was sure now. 'How things change' was her caption on the picture. It could mean almost anything, but as the other woman who'd been betrayed by Derek, I knew what prompted the caption. I knew in the way that pretty much no one else could know.

I sighed, pushing the laptop away. There it was, in black and white. I wanted to hate her. I wanted it badly. But she'd been duped by Derek as well. I knew this, even though I didn't want to believe it. I wanted to be the only victim. I wasn't. He'd hurt her as much as he'd hurt me. I could see the pain on her as clearly as if it had been my own.

I wouldn't be able to hate her. I knew that like I knew my own name. No matter how hard I tried. And if she wanted to have her kids meet mine—and if they were as sweet as they seemed—there would be no room left for hate.

At least not for Natalie Chastain.

Derek was a different matter.

I pushed my personal drama aside and pulled the grimoire closer. Running my hands over the front cover, feeling the worn leather, and the metal pieces at the corner. There was a circle of metal in the middle, and even though both metal and leather were dark and dirty with age, I could see the shape of a serpent in a figure eight formation.

A lock ran along the right side of the book.

"Oh, great. How do I open this?" I asked out loud. Now, when I was ready to look at it, I couldn't open it.

Come on, I thought. I need to find out how to do this right.

The lock clicked underneath my fingers.

"No way," I breathed. I lifted up the front cover slowly, not wanting to damage anything. Who knew how old it was? And had it heard me?

The pages were parchment, a light cream color with variations of darker spots, and there was writing on the front page. It looked... I peered more closely at it. It wasn't English. Then I blinked, and the letters shifted.

The Grimoire of the Oracle it read.

"What in the hell?" I turned the page, and the next page did the same thing—the letters shifting in front of me, so that I could read what it said.

This is the grimoire of the Oracle of Theama, written for the Oracles that come after me. We were once the Pythia, and now, we are both more and less. This is my tale, and yours as well. Share with your sisters, share so that they may light the way for those in the dark. Keep this safe. This is for the eyes of the Oracle only, and no other.

A shiver passed through me as I read the last three words.

I turned page after page, giving the grimoire time to change, although not all the pages had any writing on them. I remembered that Florry said the pages would show me what I needed when I needed it.

"Who determines that?" I asked, frowning. Of course there was no answer.

So I turned the pages until there was one with writing, and I waited for the writing to translate itself. I read about how one should choose the time to sit above the fumes carefully, as some points in the day were stronger than others. How to guard against those who would use the Oracle for ill will, or their own evil gains. How to throw bones—eww, what did that mean?—and how to read the stars.

Then the grimoire began to shift. A lot of pages were blank. I wondered if Florry had written in it. I flipped to the back, since it made sense the Oracle right before me would be the latest entries. The letters here didn't need to shift.

The last page was written in blue fountain pen, a graceful curving hand.

This is probably my last entry. I'm tired, and Goldie is really heavy on my arm. All I want is to sleep. I never knew how the end would come, but I think this is it. There are no consultants that I need to help, thank Pythia and Theama. I think this is my time. I've looked all through the grimoire, and there's nothing to guide me. Figures. Consistent to the end. Anyway, I've enjoyed it, girls, and I'm looking forward to meeting whoever comes next. If you're reading this, and you're tired, and angry, and upset and confused—let it all out, and then get to work.

It's been worth it. I have lived a life worth living.

Florence Marie Shaker

I sat back then, stunned. She'd known she was dying, or at her end. I hadn't asked her about it—she'd gone inside and I'd been back in the room at the Community Meeting place before I was even remotely close to done asking questions. I hadn't even thought to ask if it was worth it. But she said it was. I ran my hand over the page. I could feel the sincerity in the words. It radiated off the page.

Wrung out by both personal and—professional?—revelations, I heated up leftover beef stroganoff, took a long shower, and went to bed, taking the grimoire with me. I found that I didn't want to leave it downstairs, alone and vulnerable to anyone who might come knocking. Now that I knew I would need to be open for business for magical people looking for help, I didn't want anyone else to see this.

I had one more day before Logan, my first consultant, although definitely not an expert in his quest, returned, and I needed to spend the time figuring out how to help him.

When I pulled the sheets up to my chin, I felt myself sinking into sleep. Good. I was ready to rest.

But I couldn't because I was at a party, and it was loud and noisy. The room was dark, but brightly lit with chandeliers that sparkled overhead. There were many people, all dressed formally. Even though they talked, and moved and danced and drank, they all moved around a group of people off to the right. The focus of every person in the room was on the small group of people off to the side.

I walked through the crowd, looking for what or who it was that all the people in this room seemed aware of. It was hotter than Hades in here with all the people. Finally, I made my way toward the right side of the room, toward the group of people who were all facing each other in a loose circle. I couldn't see any of their faces, but I could hear the murmur of their voices.

Everyone around me could hear them as well, and I could see people straining as they danced or walked by to hear what was being said in this little circle of people. Oddly, no one seemed to notice me, even as I brushed up against people in passing.

There was a sense of… foreboding around this small group. Mostly men, but there were two flashes of color, blue and gold, that indicated women in evening gowns.

"Oh, come now, my love," I heard a woman say. "There's no need—" her voice was cut off by the ambient noise around her. Something was about to happen, about to go down, and someone was in danger. The greed, the naked greed and wanting was palpable. I could feel it like I could feel my nails digging into my hand.

I moved closer, wanting to hear this, needing to hear it —and I woke up, my eyes wide, staring at the ceiling, the gray light of dawn coming in through the window.

"Damn it!" I said, sitting up, struggling to get out of the sheet that had tangled around me.

I lay back down. Maybe I could go back to sleep.

Thirty minutes later, the full sun now shining into my room, me hot and sweaty, I knew that any further sleep wasn't going to happen. I threw back the bedclothes and went to take another shower. I took the time to put myself together. Normally, I liked to lounge in my pajamas until lunch, but something told me that today, I needed to be dressed.

Ready.

But ready for what? I put that aside. I didn't know. And stewing over what might happen wouldn't help.

Feeling slightly better, I made myself some toast and eggs and a cup of tea, and sat down, pulling the grimoire to me. Today, I needed to find something that would help me focus on how to see, or help, or offer guidance, or something, to Logan.

I flipped through the pages. There were so many blank pages. Every so often, I'd get a hint of writing, but it never fully materialized. Then I stopped, doing a double take.

There was writing on the page.

In Order To Clarify The Visions it read along the top.

This was just what I needed. Just as Florry had said. I read through the instructions. I needed to clarify my dreams, rather than visions, but maybe the two over-lapped? I'd have to take the chance. Besides, the grimoire hadn't offered anything else. I read the directions again. I didn't have any of the herbs, or anything that I needed.

I got up and paced back and forth in the kitchen. I had one day before Logan returned, before I had to get to work helping him, helping my first consultant, to find his past.

And I didn't have a clue.

You must, Goldie's voice interrupted my thoughts. *If you do not, you will be lost.*

"What does that mean?" I asked, tossing my hands up.

I will leave you.

"I'm not sure that's a bad thing. Then my life could return to normal," I said.

Nothing will ever be normal again. Even if you do live.

"What?" I shouted.

There was no answer.

"Goldie! Get your snake butt back here and answer my questions!" I glared at the glittering tattoo on my arm. "Don't you dare leave me now, not like this!"

I was alone, with no one, not even my talking tattoo, for company.

"No," I whispered. How could I be standing here, with no one to help me? To guide me? Even the Oracles of Delphi had time to prepare, time to get ready before they took on the job. Why was it so different for the Oracle of Theama? Why did I get piecemeal instructions?

I stood still for a few minutes, feeling sorry for myself. Then I looked at the grimoire, still open to the page where it listed the herbs I needed to burn in order to open my mind, to find clarity. To seek a vision that would help my consultant.

I straightened, and walked to where I had my cell phone plugged in. Taking it back to the table, I took a picture of the page.

I might be widowed, facing a future I never planned for. I might not be the only Mrs. Chastain. I might have been tossed into something that I didn't even believe was possible, much less real, with this whole Oracle thing. And this might feel like I had no choice, no say in the matter. Actually, I'd felt this way about a lot of things lately. That life was happening to me, rather than me living my life.

The idea that I was reacting to life around me was going to change. Starting right now.

There was an apothecary on the island. They were more known for teas, but they sold loose herbs. Which was what I needed. I didn't want to have to leave the island again. Taking the ferry over would be a nuisance when all I wanted was to be here and figuring out this Oracle thing.

I looked up the directions to the apothecary on my laptop. It was only about five miles away, in Vineyard Haven, another town on the island. I knew where the apothecary was, sort of, but I'd never been there before.

Twenty minutes later, I walked through the wooden door of Vineyard Apothecary and stopped. The smell of herbs permeated the air, nearly overwhelming.

It smelled wonderful. I'd never been in any herb shop ever. I wished I hadn't taken so long.

I walked further in, looking for help. "Hello?" I called.

There was bustling further in and I walked toward the sound. "Hello?" I called again.

A woman came out from a doorway. "Hello!" she said, smiling broadly. She was as short as I was, petite with rounded hips and waving curly brown hair. "Can I help you?"

"I'm looking for some loose herbs," I said. "I… I want to make my own incense, I guess you'd call it." I wasn't going to tell her I was looking for help with visions.

"Oh, I can definitely help you there," she said. "I'm Nayla. Do you have a list?"

"I do," I said, taking out my phone.

"Come on back. We have a separate section for the loose herbs. Do you have a burner?"

"A what?" I asked.

"A burner. For your herbs," Nayla said, smiling invitingly.

"No, I guess I need that, too," I said.

"Well, show me your list, and I'll get you an burner for loose herbs," Nayla said. "It takes a little longer for the burner to heat, but it really allows the herbs to expand and give off a good scent."

"Okay," I said as I pulled my phone out of my purse, and read off the list.

Thyme

Amaranth

Artemisia Vulgaris

Dandelion

Myrrh

Desert Sage

Nayla bustled around, putting together the herbs in cloth drawstring bags. "I'm doing enough for four or five burnings," Nayla said, her back to me. "See how you like it, and if you do, we can talk about doing more of a bulk purchase the next time you're in."

It seemed odd to be putting together herbs to help me with magic, with this nice woman helping me like it was nothing at all.

"Can I help you with anything else?" Nayla asked.

"No. I think this will be all," I said.

"Well, all right, then. Let's get you rung up." She chattered as she took my card, bagging up the herbs and the incense burner. "You'll have to let me know what happens," Nayla said.

"I'm sorry?" I asked. I was thinking about what would happen when I burned all this. Would anything happen at all?

"With your incense mix. If you like it. We always like to hear what customers think." She smiled broadly. "If you give it a positive review, we can make some up, so that it's already mixed for you."

"Oh, okay. Yes, I will," I said. I walked out and before I knew it, I was back out in the parking lot, bag in hand, and getting into my car.

Until this moment, everything seemed more… distant. Not real. I mean, it was real, because things had been happening to me nonstop. The bracelet, or should I say, Goldie. Logan Gentry showing up on my doorstep. Meeting Florry. The grimoire.

But with this herbal recipe, if I did the spell as it was listed in the grimoire, this was my first step to accepting all that had happened.

Because it was my step. *My* action.

There would be no going back.

When I got home, I drifted back in as though in a dream. I set my purchases on the counter, and opened up the book.

"All right," I said. "Let's do this."

I'd made my choice.

I followed the directions, crumbling the herbs one at a time into the small burner. Then I lit the tea light that sat underneath the burner. According to Nayla, as well as the directions that came with the burner, it would take a while for the burner to heat, and for the herbs to begin to release their scent and their powers. That last bit came from the grimoire. The grimoire entry cautioned patience. That it would be better to wait, and allow the herbs to fully burn.

After a time, I could see that smoke was drifting upwards, swirling in a whitish gray plume. I checked the grimoire again, and took a deep breath. Carefully, I moved the burner closer, so that I could lean over it without having to reach too far. One last glance at the grimoire, and—I stopped, seeing a scribble off to the side I hadn't noticed before. I peered at it, trying to decipher the tiny writing.

Tie back long hair. Burnt hair ruins the spell.

I burst out laughing. So much for mysticism. I hurried to my junk drawer, looking for a hair band. I quickly pulled my hair back. I agreed with whomever had written the warning. Burnt hair would ruin everything, and the smell would take forever to get out of my kitchen.

Then I was back over the burner, leaning over, and inhaling the herbs. They smelled good, with a bit of a spicy tang. I took another deep breath, and began to chant the words that were written along with the herbal recipe.

"Break the wall and expand the crack,

Clear my way; send vision back.

All that blocks me now be gone,

Make dark to light just like the dawn."

There were several variations, with different hand-writing changing the spell via a word here or there. That actually made me feel better. It meant Oracles before me had done this, and it had worked. Then they'd worked on improving it.

I said it three times, just as the grimoire said to. I closed my eyes, and focused on allowing the answer to show itself to me. Another suggestion from the grimoire. Then I breathed in the tangy scent of the herbs, and waited.

It was the party scene I'd seen in my dream last night. I could see all the people dancing and moving about the room, all focused on the small group of people off to the side. This time, I got closer to the small group. Like before, I could see blue and gold evening dresses, and I heard the soft laughter of women's voices. I was able to see more clearly this time, and I could see five men. Or rather, there were four men who were all focused on the fifth man.

This fifth man was talking, to one of the women, I thought. He was tall, his hair cut closely around his head. It was a medium brown, somewhere in between blond and black hair, but more dark than fair. The four men and two women all bent toward this fifth man, and I allowed myself to look more closely at the men.

They were not friends to the fifth man. They didn't like him at all—in fact, at least one, maybe two of the men hated him. They were... I had to close my eyes and really focus, because this was getting muddled and blurry. They wanted something from him, wanted it badly.

With an abrupt jerk, I was out of the dream world, out of the party, and back in my kitchen. The burner of herbs was nearly empty. The kitchen smelled wonderful, much like the apothecary shop.

"Okay," I said, getting up to get a glass of water. I drank the entire thing, and filled it again. Once I did, I sat down to consider what I'd seen.

How did this fit in with my current gig? With what Logan wanted? I hadn't seen him in any of my dreams, or in any way at all. How was I supposed to find his past when I couldn't even find how he'd lost it? I raced up to my room, finding the notebook I'd made notes in before, and added to them. I didn't want to lose any of the details. When you had nothing, you didn't know what might end up being important.

I spent the rest of the day thumbing through the pages of the grimoire, looking for some way to focus my visions, or dreams, or whatever so that I could help Logan. What had Goldie said? All would be lost if I didn't help Logan find what he was after.

I wasn't sure what that meant, mostly because Goldie hadn't told me anything more. But I had seen more of the dream of the man in danger. I'd know to keep an eye out for him.

Maybe he was my next consultant.

None of which helped Logan, or me.

After flipping the pages of the grimoire, some of them began to show words. I read about previous Oracles, fascinated. These were more personal notes, like the one from Florry. I'd gotten off track, reading about the former Oracles. I knew now why I could see Florry. When the bracelet passed from one Oracle to the next, the previous Oracle was visible to the new Oracle. To help her. To guide her. That much had been shown to me.

"I don't feel all that guided," I said to my ceiling. "I could use a little more."

As was becoming the norm, no one replied. You'd think with all the help I supposedly had, someone would say something—but nope. It was quiet as any tomb in here.

I waited for close to an hour for... what, I wasn't sure. But nothing happened. So I made myself some dinner, and cleaned up the kitchen.

Logan would be back tomorrow, wanting answers. I didn't have any, but I had a burning spell that might help me see something for him. I took the grimoire upstairs with me, sleeping with it in my bed again. I didn't want to let it get too far away.

I wasn't sure that was healthy, but I wasn't going to fight my instinct. It needed to be near me.

When I got up the next morning, I felt better. If I'd dreamed, I couldn't remember. I was hot, like ridiculously hot, as was the norm every day now. Yay, me. But I was better. Not entirely ready, but better. I was going to solve this, I hoped. Then I was going to give up the damn bracelet, and let someone else be the

Oracle. But since I didn't want to suffer whatever fate it was Goldie had hinted at, I'd take care of Logan. I'd seen his back, I'd felt his pain when he talked about waking up in the desert, and then shifting without understanding why. He deserved answers.

That, however, would be it for me. I would not be the Oracle. This job was not my choice, my destiny, or anything other than a pain in the butt for me. That had become clear to me last night, while I lay in bed thinking over everything I'd learned. I'd take care of this concern, and then I would decline to do anything else. There had to be some choice allowed, right?

I made a pot of tea, and sat down to wait, pleased that I'd made my decision. The last two weeks of someone else calling the shots had bothered me more than I wished.

When the doorbell rang, I was ready. I could tell it was Logan even before I walked through the vestibule. His tall form was unmistakable.

I swung the door open, not sure what I'd find.

He smiled.

"Come in," I said. "We need to talk."

CHAPTER EIGHT

"You look..." Logan stopped, and looked at me.

I had to turn my face away. His gaze made me feel exposed. I felt like he saw everything. And I was overwhelmed with the sense of animal wildness in him, the feeling that I was being evaluated by a predator.

"What?" I asked when he didn't continue his sentence.

"Different," Logan finished.

"That's it? That wait, all that build up, and all you can come up with is different?" I asked, smiling.

He gave me a rueful grin. "It wasn't very descriptive, but it's the best I can manage. I can't find the word. Something, though, is very different about you."

"Good or bad?" I asked as I walked toward the kitchen.

"Good," Logan replied promptly. "You were nervous and jumpy the last time I saw you. What's happened in the last two days?"

"Would you like something to drink?" I asked.

"Coffee if you have it," he said.

"I have tea, but it won't take long for coffee," I said. Derek had been the coffee drinker. The kids and I all drank tea. I'd had more coffee recently than I normally did. I pulled out the small coffee maker from its corner on the counter, and took my time measuring out the coffee that was in the back of the cabinet.

"So what happened?" Logan asked.

I leaned against the island where he sat on the other side. "Well, I've been doing some work on figuring out more about being the Oracle."

"And?"

"There's a lot to it. I'm nowhere near figuring it out. But I have a more solid footing," I said, and found that I was smiling.

"And you're not going to get into the details, are you?" Logan asked.

"No, I don't think I am," I said slowly. He didn't need to know everything, even though I was excited about all that I'd discovered. "What you need to know is that you are right, much as I hate to say it."

"I'm glad to hear it. I'll tell you, just to get it out of the way, that I'm often right," Logan said.

"Whatever," I rolled my eyes. "I *am* the Oracle, no matter what I think about it, and I have some ideas on how to help you find your answers."

I didn't imagine the look of relief on his face.

"That's great," he said. "I'm glad for you. So what's next?"

It was kind of a letdown to have done all that I'd done over the past couple of days, and have the object of my efforts, in a sense, just nod and move on.

But I stopped myself.

I was doing this for him, sure, but more than that, I was trying to figure out what to do next for me. Not for

Logan, or any other consultant who might show up on my doorstep. Logan would disappear after I helped him, but I'd still be here, with my armband tattoo, with Goldie, and apparently Florry from time to time. Until I passed this on to someone else. In order to do that, I had to solve Logan's request.

Straightening my shoulders, I shrugged off my disappointment at Logan's response. His response wasn't the validation I needed. It was time for me to stop worrying about looking for that validation outwardly. I'd been doing that my entire life, I realized, caught in what my gran would call a Home Truth. Looking for validation as a wife, as a mother, as the person who held it all together. That was part of the reason I was so off balance. I hadn't been holding it together at all.

And yet somehow, things were still all right. That would take more time to dissect than I had at the moment. I shook my head to clear it, and smiled at Logan. "I want to do a burning spell with you, so I can focus on what it is you're seeking," I said.

"Okay. What do you need me to do?" He didn't hesitate.

I laughed then. "Just sit there and focus on the question you want me to answer."

The coffee pot beeped softly, letting me know that it was done. I got him a cup, and waited while Logan fixed his coffee.

He drank deeply, sighing as he lowered the cup. "I needed that."

"Was it a difficult client?" I asked, remembering that his note had said he was leaving to do work for a client. I topped off my tea from the pot I'd made earlier.

God, was it really only two days ago that Logan had left me that note? It felt like a century.

He frowned. "Well, that was part of what I wanted to talk with you about. I think the client recognized me."

"What?"

Logan nodded. "When I delivered his item—"

"What item?"

His eyes slid away. "I find things for people. On commission."

Something didn't make sense. "Okay. Is that bad? I mean, people lose things all the time."

One corner of Logan's lips lifted. "Well, it's a little different when you're dealing with supes. I find magical items that my clients request. Sometimes I have to get them via less than aboveboard methods."

It took me a moment. "You're a thief?"

"Not a thief. I acquire things."

I rolled my eyes. "Yes, I'm sure that's what the local burglar says when the police catch him."

Logan shrugged. "Tomato, tomahto. When I woke up in the desert, and had no idea who I was, or how to make sure I could eat, I found that I was good at finding things. Like, if you lost a ring twenty years ago, and you asked me to find it, I would." He shrugged again. "Mark, that was the shifter who helped me?" He looked at me to see if I remembered that part of his story.

I nodded.

"Mark said it was obviously a gift, and it would be foolish for me to ignore it. There I was, beaten and bruised and broke. I've been a finder ever since." His green eyes bored into mine. "But that doesn't matter. What matters is that my client this time nearly choked when he saw me."

"I take it that he was not happy to see you?"

"I don't know," Logan leaned back, taking another sip of coffee. "He hid his surprise right away. But not so fast that I didn't notice it."

"Did you ask him about it?"

He shook his head. "No. I didn't want to give it away that I'd seen his response. What if he's part of the reason I'm like this? That I've lost all my life but the past seven years?"

"Who would do this to you?"

"That's what you're going to tell me," Logan said.

I felt the weight of his expectations land on me like an anvil in the cartoons I used to watch on Saturday mornings. "I'll do my best. You do know that the Oracle doesn't hand you an answer that solves everything easy peasy, right? I've been reading, and a lot of times, the answer isn't always clear."

"It's better than the nothing I've got now," Logan said.

"Make sure he pays you for all these shenanigans," I heard behind me.

I whipped around. "Florry?"

"What?" Logan asked.

I held up a hand to forestall any further questions from Logan while I sorted this out. "Florry? Where are you?"

"I'm right here," she said, her voice sounding cross. After a moment, she appeared, leaning against the counter off to the right, smoking a cigarette. It didn't smell, thank goodness. I hated the smell of smoking. But I guessed you took your habits with you when you passed over to the other side.

As before, she was in a white nightie with flowers, and a purple housecoat over the nightgown. White fuzzy slippers, rather than blue, were on her feet. They were in better shape than the blue ones.

"What did you say?" I asked.

"I said, make sure he pays you. I haven't heard any mention of how he plans to compensate you for your services in all this friendly sharing." She made a face as she blew a plume of smoke from her mouth.

"Oh, isn't that interesting," I said, trying not to let Logan know what we were talking about.

"Is someone here?" Logan asked, looking between me and where Florry stood. He obviously couldn't see her.

"Call me your spiritual guide," Florry said before I could respond.

"Yes," I said, not taking my eyes from her. "It's my spiritual guide."

Logan's eyes narrowed, but he only nodded. "Do you need a minute?"

"No, boy, we're fine." Florry rolled her eyes. "Tell him that. That you're fine."

"No, I'm fine," I said, turning back to him. "My guide shows up at will."

"That's handy," Logan said.

"It is, sort of," I smiled. "My… guide is quite helpful. When she chooses to be." I glared at Florry.

Florry made a choking sound that dissolved into wheezy laughter. I swear, she was the poster child for every little old lady stereotype.

I took a breath. "Sorry for the interruption, Logan. One of the things that we haven't discussed is the matter of compensation," I said. This was hard for me. I was used to just doing for others, no further questions asked.

Another thing that would need to change.

"What?" Logan's eyes widened.

"Compensation. When the Oracle gives a consultant assistance, the consultant needs to make an offering to the Oracle."

He didn't say anything.

"Oh, yeah, we weren't expecting that," Florry commented, her tone dry and caustic.

I resisted the urge to tell her to hush. I didn't want Logan to know that I hadn't even thought about this until Florry brought it up. But given the fact that I was heading into retirement with less than I thought I'd have, the fact that I should expect payment for my services was a comfort I hadn't planned on.

I stopped myself. Why was I thinking about this? I was going to give this up the moment I finished helping Logan.

"Would you prefer service or tangible goods?" Logan asked calmly.

"Oh, this is good," Florry said. "Tell him service."

"What?" I turned to her.

"Do it, girl. I'll explain later." She made a shooing motion with her hands.

"Service," I said, feeling a little silly at how formal the one word came out.

Logan nodded. "Service it is, then. I'm at your disposal. We can work out the terms later, if that is your preference."

"Exactly what we need," Florry said with great satisfaction. "Now do your thing, girl, and let's see what we see."

I almost asked her how she knew what I was planning, but I stopped myself. I smiled at Logan. "Excellent. Thank you. We will manage the specifics later. " I took a breath. "I want to try something with you, something I've been experimenting with myself. If you'll allow me?"

"You're the Oracle," he said. "Whatever you need to do."

Something clicked in me then. It took away the uncomfortable feeling I had about being more formal than I'd been with Logan, and my general discomfort with this entire situation.

I *was* the Oracle. And even though I wanted to find a way to get out of this, with my life relatively intact— right now, I was the Oracle. It was time that I started acting like it.

"I know that, but this is not a solo process," I said. "This needs both of us to work." I didn't know how I knew, but I knew he had to be a part of my attempt at seeing.

"Whatever you feel is best," he said.

"Okay, give me a moment," I said, and I brought out the burner I'd used before, as well as a small bag of the herbal mix I'd gotten from the apothecary. I lit the candle, and poured the herbs into the burner. "We need to let it warm, and once the smoke starts to rise, we'll clasp hands and inhale the fumes."

"You did this before? What did you see?" Logan's face was open, curious.

"Things I didn't expect to," I said, staying deliberately vague. I realized that I could do this, and it would be seen as just me being the Oracle, that people wouldn't question me.

That could be good.

If I planned to keep on being the Oracle, it would be good. But I wasn't planning on being like Florry, the Oracle until I died. No. Just help Logan and pass it on. I pushed all these thoughts aside in order to focus on the consultant in front of me.

Logan and I sat quietly, both drinking our drinks as the herbs began to heat and the smell of the mixture permeated the kitchen. When the smoke was visible, and pooling above the burner, I set aside my cup. God, I hoped this would work.

"You're on the right track," Florry said, still leaning against the counter.

I ignored her. If she was still here afterwards, we could talk then. When it was just the two of us.

I moved around to the other side of the island, sitting on the barstool next to Logan. I also moved the burner so that it was between us. "Okay, take my hands, and close your eyes. I want you to focus on the question that brought you here as you breathe in the herbs."

"I can't think of much else," Logan muttered.

"Well, good," I said, smiling briefly.

He reached out, and I took his hands. The feel of his hands, warm and slightly calloused, sent an electric shock through me. Calm down, I told myself. You need to focus on the job, not how nice his hands feel.

But they did feel nice.

I closed my eyes, and leaned in over the burner, inhaling deeply. Across from me, I heard Logan inhale as well.

Show me his past, I thought. *Let me help him find his way.* I inhaled once, then twice, taking the time to stretch out my breath, to allow myself to relax into my breathing. Kind of like the yoga and wine nights I'd gone to with Shelly.

But this time, I didn't just count the seconds before the yoga ended and the wine began. This time, I felt myself fall into a darkness. It wasn't scary, oddly enough. I wasn't afraid, at least, and given recent events, that was a good thing. Logan's hands in mine were a talisman, a touchstone that kept me grounded and focused on finding the answer to my question.

Show me his past, I thought again.

The darkness continued, and then with a flash, I was back in the room of the party I'd been dreaming about. The people were the same, or at least similar, and my attention was drawn to the grouping of people on the right. Only this time, the air in the room was… different.

It was full of magic.

Like in the movies, when you can see the sparkles that indicate something otherworldly is happening. White and gold and light pastel colors, the sparkles moved around the room, with no direction.

The entire room was magic. This was something that had happened, or was happening, in a magical setting.

Unlike the movies, however, this was not all good and happy magic. There was ill intent moving throughout the crowd. I felt it the most when I looked at the group of men and women that had captured my attention from the first time I'd seen this room. I wondered why I could see the magical part of this now, when I hadn't before.

The ill will was focused on the tall man with his back to me. The four men around him weren't his friends, even though they all talked and laughed as though they were.

One of the women put a hand on the man's shoulder, and he started to turn.

My heart leapt in anticipation—I'd finally get to see his face, so I would know who to look for.

My vision went dark, and I couldn't see anything but the darkness behind my closed eyes.

"No," I said out loud. *Show me his face! I need to see it so I can move on.*

Nothing. I couldn't see a damn thing.

Show me Logan Gentry' past, I thought. *Let me help him at least.*

Still nothing.

I was very aware of Logan's hands in mine, but hard as I tried, I couldn't see anything else.

I sighed, not ready to open my eyes.

And then I was upstairs, in my bedroom. It was night, and the window was open. The curtains blew softly with a light breeze. I saw myself in bed. My heart raced. Something bad was about to happen, but I couldn't see—

My eyes flew open. Logan was holding my hands, his eyes closed, his face solemn. His cheekbones were in sharp relief, his scar stark against his skin, his face angular and breathtaking.

I let go of his hands.

Logan's eyes flew open. "What did you see?"

"Don't lie," Florry said. "I can tell you didn't see what you wanted. But one of the things about the Oracles is that we don't lie. Things may not be clear right away, but you'll get clarity. Eventually," she added.

"I didn't see anything that gets me closer to your past. What I did see was a mystery I think I need to solve so that I can help you," I said. Thank goodness Florry popped in with a response.

Logan frowned. "That's not very helpful."

"That's part of being an Oracle!" Florry snapped. "We don't get answers all nice and neat and tied up in a bow!"

I liked that she was indignant for me. "One of the things I've learned is that answers aren't always straightforward," I said to Logan. "But I am assured, by those that were Oracles before me, that the truth becomes clear. There are reasons that things are shown as they are," I said. Where that had come from, I didn't know, but I knew it was true. I leaned over and blew out the tea light beneath the burner. Whatever else was going on, I knew this session of attempting to see was done.

Logan nodded and sighed. "I've never met any sooth-sayers that were able to come out and give a direct answer." He smiled but his smile was tinged with sadness. "Which kind of makes things difficult for me. I've been looking for answers for over seven years. It won't kill me to wait a little longer."

"Logan, can we go back to what you said about the recent client before we did this?" I waved a hand to indicate the burner. "You said that you find things—"

"You called me a thief," he interrupted, one eyebrow raising.

"Is that the truth?" I asked.

His shoulders moved up toward his ears, and then he deliberately dropped them. "I could be called a thief," he said carefully. "But I evaluate each job, and decide if it's worth crossing the line."

"What does that mean?" I asked. I hated all this double speak.

"It means I look at the person I might have to liberate an item from, and how they might have gotten it in the first place," Logan said, and now there was humor in his voice. "Not everyone in the magical world is a good guy."

"I'm learning that," I said, thinking about the magic that was anything but good I'd seen in my vision. When I looked around the kitchen, I noted that Florry had disappeared. Well. That wasn't very helpful. Maybe after Logan left, I could yell until she showed up again. Or maybe there was a section in the grimoire that would appear about the basic How To's of being the damn Oracle. Because the surprises were getting old. Even as I felt more comfortable, I felt—the sound of the doorbell made me jump. "What now?" I asked as I got up.

CHAPTER NINE

*a*s I opened the vestibule door, I could see the dark blue uniforms of the police. "Great," I said.

"Is everything all right?" Logan was behind me.

"Don't do that," I said crossly. "Don't sneak up behind me. I didn't even hear you leave the kitchen."

"Part of the job," he said quietly. "The cops?"

"Yes," I couldn't contain my irritation. "Because of Ash."

"The guy who had the bracelet?" His humor was back. "The Indiana Jones look alike?"

I was not amused. "Yes. You can forget you ever heard me say that. Can you go back to the kitchen?" I was acutely aware of how this was going to look. They'd met me while I was reporting the disappearance of a man I'd just met; now I was here with another man, a big, handsome man, only a couple of days later—good lord. I could hear the gossip.

Well, it was no one's business but mine. I yanked open the door as I pasted a smile on my face. "Officers," I said. "What can I do for you?"

Andy Dentwhistle, along with Scott Trenton glowering over his shoulder, stood on my front porch.

"Hey, Wynter," he said. "We came by because we have some more questions for you. May we come in?"

"Sure," I said, stepping back. "Of course." I turned and walked toward the kitchen. "Would you close both doors, please?" I asked over my shoulder. I didn't slow down.

Once in the kitchen, I leaned against the far counter. Both men came in, Andy looking less comfortable than Scott. Scott just looked annoyed, and as though he was trying to be threatening. "Have a seat," I said. I gestured at the island.

I noted that only my cup was on the island. The burner had been moved to the center, as though it was nothing more than a pleasant decoration. "Would you like some coffee, or tea?" I asked.

"You have company?" Scott Trenton asked.

"I do," I said. "But I don't see how that's important."

"It's important if we say it is," Scott shot back.

"Hey," Logan's deep voice came from the living room. "Wynter, are you all right?" He looked around as though he hadn't seen the officers before. "What's going on?"

"Who are you?" Scott asked, taking a step toward Logan.

"I'm Logan Gentry, a friend of the family. I've been traveling, but when I came back to the States, I heard about Derek, and came to offer my condolences," Logan said, walking toward Scott with his hand out. "He was too young."

"That he was," Andy said, watching Logan and Scott shake hands. "What is it you do, Mr. Gentry?"

"I'm a curator for private collectors," Logan said, big smile still in place. "They hire me to find pieces for them. You know collectors. There's never enough time for them. Which is good for guys like me." He stepped to the side and shook Andy's hand.

"We need to speak to her alone," Scott said.

"Wynter?" Logan looked at me.

"Logan is a good friend. I'm fine with him being here," I said, directing my comments to Andy.

"You sure about that? Him being a friend of your late husband and all?" Scott asked. He really had a nasty smile.

"What are you insinuating?" I asked.

"The fact that the night we met you, you went back to a hotel with a man you met not an hour before," Scott said.

I could tell that he'd been waiting to say that. The little weasel. My hand itched to slap the smug right out of him.

"Am I missing something here?" I looked between the two officers, letting my gaze land on Andy. "What does Ash have to do with Derek? I don't see the connection?"

"It's been what, six months? You know what they say," Logan said, jumping into the conversation. "Those who were happy often find a new partner quickly.

Happiness attracts happiness," he added, a smile on his face as he stared a hole into Scott Trenton.

It was petty, but I was glad to see Scott wither a little under Logan's harsh glare. I wasn't a violent person, but Scott Trenton's comments were beginning to grate on me.

"Ashton Flint has nothing to do with Derek. We actually came here to show you a photo. The drawing you helped the sketch artist make got a hit, and I wanted to see if this was the guy," Andy said.

Scott pulled out a photo from the leather portfolio he carried and set it on the island.

I hadn't even noticed the portfolio in Scott's hands. I guess I was too focused on his negative intensity to see anything else. His anger, his negativity—it was all around him like a storm cloud. Interesting. I'd never seen that around anyone before. I moved closer for a look, crossing my arms in front of me.

It was Ash, although quite a bit younger. "That's him," I said. "But I don't think this is a recent picture."

"It's not," Andy said. "It's about ten years old."

"Is Ash his real name?" I asked.

Andy nodded. "It is. He's an archeologist, and he's been involved in some legal concerns in Europe."

"He sounds a bit shady," Logan said. "Good thing he skipped out on you." He gave me a nod.

"You told him?" Andy looked from me to Logan and back again.

"Of course," I said. "I have nothing to hide." I looked right at Officer Weasel Scott Trenton as I spoke. "Have you located him?"

"No," Andy shook his head, handing the photo back to Scott, who tucked it into the portfolio. "I wish we did. But at least now, we know without a doubt who we're looking for." He nodded at me. "That's all we needed, Wynter. Sorry for bothering you."

He turned and walked back toward the door. Scott looked up from fiddling with the portfolio. "You still need to stay here in town," he said.

"Why?" I shot back. "I didn't do anything."

"Scott," Andy stopped in the doorway and glared at his partner. "We're done. Thanks, Wynter," he said. "We can see ourselves out."

"Make sure you shut both the doors," Logan said, grinning broadly.

Neither of us spoke until we heard the bang of both doors. I sagged against the island.

"What is it they think you did? At least, the shorter guy, the mean one," Logan said.

"Who knows? Scott Trenton thinks I'm guilty of all sorts of things. He's not from here. Andy has known me all his life, and so if he thinks I'm guilty, he's hiding it better."

"They both suck at the good cop, bad cop routine," Logan said with a sniff. "That's what they're doing, although that Scott guy might be more into it than the other one."

"Enough about them," I waved a hand, consigning Officers Dentwhistle and Trenton to another time. "You were talking about your client?"

Logan walked out toward the living room, looking out the window. "It was weird. I got the commission request, and I agreed on it, and the item he wanted was pretty easily sourced. So I showed up at the address he gave to deliver it. And when he opened the door, I could see the shock on his face. He took a step back, like he was nervous, and he said, K, and then he stopped."

"He said the letter 'k'?" I asked.

"That's what it sounded like. I introduced myself, and he was nervous, glancing at me like he was afraid I'd sprout horns and wings, or something. It was one of the most uncomfortable client meetings I've ever had."

"So what do you want to do?" I asked.

"Will you go back to see him with me? While I won't tell him you're the Oracle, he may not lie right to my face. There's something about you now, a presence you didn't have before. It could be useful." He stopped. "Because I really don't want to be lied to again," Logan said, his words ending in a growl.

"Well, if you talked to me like that, I'd lie to your face, too, just to get you out of my house."

"Or pepper spray me," Logan said, laughing.

"Or that. If you recall, that didn't make you leave either." I laughed with him.

"Are you carrying the pepper spray and the Taser?" he asked, his demeanor serious.

I nodded. "Everywhere I go now. Just in case."

"Good. I don't really know all the protection in place for the Oracle—"

"That makes two of us," I grumbled.

"But it's better to be overly prepared."

"Based on your experience?" I asked.

"Something like that," Logan said with a smile.

"Ah. Okay, so you want me to come and see this client of yours," I said, getting us back on track.

"Peter Dunleavy. I don't recall working with him before, but seven years isn't all that long in this business."

"What does that mean?" I asked.

"Well, most people in the magical world live longer lives than what is considered a normal human life time."

"Oh," I hadn't considered that. One more thing to ask Florry about. "How long do you think you'll live?"

He shrugged. "Animals usually live shorter lives than humans, but I'm both. Animal and human. Mark— that's my friend, Mark Tattersall, the shifter who found me in the desert, he says that I'll be able to tell that I'm aging when it's more work to shift."

"It's not work now?" I asked. A part of me couldn't believe I was asking about someone turning into an animal like it was no big thing, but I found this idea fascinating.

"No," Logan shook his head. "I had to think about it at first, but now, I can shift easily."

"Well, good. Please tell me to move if you're about to shift," I said. "When do you want to see this client?"

"What's your afternoon look like?"

I hesitated. I didn't have any plans. Shelly had left several voice messages for me. I would need to call her, probably tonight, before she came over banging on my door and demanding answers. I was lucky she'd held off until now. "I can do it this afternoon. Where is he?"

"In New Bedford, believe it or not. He's close. We can take the ferry over."

"Okay, that will work," I said, nodding. It wasn't a long ferry ride, only about forty minutes. That would give me plenty of time. "I have something I have to do tonight."

"Great. Thank you," Logan said. "I have an errand to run, and then when I get back, we'll go. Does that work?"

"Yes," I said. I'd call Shelly once he left. Better to get this out of the way. There was so much weirdness going on, I didn't need her barging in here. I'd been avoiding her, but with me being at the police station, she was bound to have heard about it. I needed to head her off at the pass. Although that was one of the things I loved about her—her take charge attitude and her willingness to forge ahead no matter what.

"Okay, I'll see you soon. And I'll close both doors behind me," he added.

Once he was gone, I picked up the phone and dialed Shelly's number.

She answered on the second ring. "It's a good thing you called me. I was about to come and see you."

"You know, you're not supposed to make that sound like a threat," I said.

"I wanted to make sure that you were all right," Shelly said, her voice softening. "It hasn't been that long since you found out about Derek."

"No, but I'm okay," I said.

"So what's been going on? Been to any cop shops lately?"

"Oh, god, you heard?" I groaned.

"Everyone's heard, honey."

"This is what I get. I go out, go dancing, and decide, what the hell? He's cute and sexy and he seems to like me. Then I come out of the bathroom at his hotel room, and he's gone!"

Shelly laughed. "This is not what you get. You just happened to choose Mr. Wrong and Wrong Time to sow your wild oats with. Have the police found him?"

"No," I said. "I don't know the guy well, or anything, but I liked him. I hope he's okay." The nagging feeling that he hadn't just bailed on me, but was removed against his will had been growing. I kept telling myself it wasn't just my vanity talking.

"They'll find him," Shelly said. "I'm just sorry your first foray into the dating world went so sideways."

"You and me both," I said.

"Have you talked to her?"

I knew exactly who Shelly referred to. "No. The kids are coming over this weekend. They want to talk about making contact. They want to meet the kids."

"They're not mad at her?" Shelly was surprised.

"They are. Madder than I am, actually," I said.

"And why is it you're not mad anymore? It hasn't been that long since I talked to you," Shelly demanded.

"Because I'm following her online, and I don't think she knew," I said. "If she didn't know, she's just like me. Fooled. Duped. Lied to."

"Rich," Shelly said.

"Well, there is that. But while she got most of the life insurance, I got all the proceeds from the business. It's in a trust for the kids, and an annuity for me, so I don't starve or have to live in a box under a bridge, but she can't touch that."

"If she tries, I'll get you a lawyer," Shelly said. "I have a couple of old cranks who love this kind of case."

"You're calling someone else an old crank?" I asked, laughing.

"Why don't I come over and we'll have some tea and chat?" Shelly asked.

"I can't. I have some business to take care of today. But I'm free tonight. You want to come over for dinner?"

"I'll bring the dinner. You make a salad and some bread," Shelly replied.

"Great. I'll see you at six, then," I said. That would give me and Logan enough time. It wasn't even ten o'clock yet. We could make the ten forty-five ferry if his errand didn't take long.

We hung up, and I went upstairs to tidy myself up, and get ready for a day out. I added yelling for Florry to future business. There wasn't enough time for me to get into it with her on all the topics I wanted to discuss. Normally, this would make me all itchy and anxious, but now, I knew that I'd see her soon enough, and get the answers I wanted. Well, maybe. Florry was pretty good at hedging and disappearing when she wanted to.

The doorbell pulled me from my musings when it rang at a quarter after ten. It was Logan, back from his errand. He drove us to the ferry dock. It was a gorgeous day. Once Logan drove onto the ferry, I got out, tilting my head toward the sun.

"We can sit on the deck," he said.

Together, we walked up to the observation deck.

When Derek died, the kids had talked to me about moving, to somewhere smaller, somewhere not an island, but I'd refused. Not only because this was my family home, and I'd lived here all my life, but because I loved being close to the water. When you lived on an island, your world was influenced by the sea. I couldn't imagine being away from her. The sound of her, the smell, the storms—I loved it. All of it.

Once on the observation deck, I leaned over the railing. The water had that lovely blue-green color to it that you saw in the summer at times. I inhaled the sharp, briny smell. It made me feel better.

"This is a really beautiful place," Logan said next to me.

"I love it," I said. "I've lived here all my life."

"Really?" he asked.

"Yes. The house I'm in was my family home." Which was the same situation as Florry, I realized with a start. Her place in Kansas. She said it was a family home, too. Was that part of being the Oracle? Being a woman who had roots in her community? Who understood the importance of community? Yet one more thing to ask Florry. While I was musing over this coincidence, another sound interrupted my thoughts.

You are a child of many things, but you are also a child of the sea, a deep rumbling voice said. It was so deep that my ears rang.

"What?" I whispered.

You are a child of the sea. You have crossed over me many times, but this is the first time that we may speak, the voice continued.

"Wynter? Is something wrong?" Logan asked me, moving closer.

"I need to sit down," I whispered, reaching out for his arm. "Please." My hand gripped his arm tightly.

He put a hand on my back and brought me to one of the benches away from the other passengers. "Wynter, what is it?"

"In a minute," I got out. *Who are you?* I thought. Because this was definitely not Goldie. In fact, Goldie had been suspiciously quiet all morning.

I am Tethys, guardian of the sea. And we women, all women, are of the sea. Most never learn this, never learn to speak of the sea. To speak with it. You have always known of your ties to me. I am happy to speak with you, daughter.

You know this about me? I thought, my eyes closing. In my head, I could see a large, green shape in the dark depths of the water. It flowed with the ocean, the green tendrils disappearing into the deep. It was all very opaque, unclear, except for the dark golden eyes. Those blazed like the sun, made all the brighter by the darkness around them. Around her. Tethys. *What do you want from me?*

Nothing, Tethys said, and there was a hint of laughter and danger in that one word. *I choose to speak to you because you can now hear. I have chosen to deliver a message, young Oracle. There is a reason all things are hidden. They are hidden until it is time for them to be revealed. The sea is the mistress of this. Everything is hidden for a time, until it is not. Sometimes, many of your human years are required for things to be revealed. Trust that the sea shows what she wishes.*

Okay, I thought. *I have no idea what you mean.*

You will, young one. You will. I welcome you.

She was gone as quickly as I'd sensed her. I opened my eyes, and took a deep breath. "That was weird."

"What? You got all pale. I was worried you were sick or something," Logan asked. "You don't get seasick, do you?"

I laughed. "No. I've lived on the Vineyard all my life, Logan. No, it was a message."

"From who? Was it about me?" His gaze sharpened.

"No, I don't think so. I think it's more of Oracle stuff versus Logan stuff." I had no idea what the message was about, honestly. I really needed a guidebook. This was getting ridiculous. Could anyone magic just talk to me, invade my head space? I'd have to find a way to stop that, if so. "I forgot to ask. Did you finish your errand?" I turned to Logan. "And thank you for helping me. Sorry you thought I was about to barf all over you."

"That would have made this trip a lot less pleasant," he said. "Yes, I did finish my errand. Hopefully we won't need it, but it's better to be prepared."

"Need what?" I asked, the alarm bells going off in my head.

"It doesn't matter. We may not need it, and if we don't, I'd rather not talk about it." Logan frowned.

"Do I need to worry about this?" I asked.

"No. It's just a little insurance," Logan made a movement with one of his hands. It was clear he didn't want to talk about it further.

"All right," I said. Normally, I wouldn't let this go. But something told me to leave it be. I went with it. "I'll trust you."

"Good," he said, looking out over the water. "You want to talk about what just happened with you?"

"No, you're just going to have to trust me," I said.

Logan looked down at me then. "Looks like we're going to have to trust each other. I can do that if you can."

"I can," I said. "Besides, do we have a choice?"

He laughed softly. "No, we don't. Although at this point, it's a little late to be worrying about it, in my opinion. But if you need to say it out loud, to be sure, to give our word to one another, I'm fine with that."

"My word, then," I said.

"Mine as well," Logan said.

We didn't speak much as the ferry got closer to New Bedford. When the dock was in view, we walked back to the car. I was thinking about Tethys, and the whole idea of trusting a man I'd only known a week. Was this wise? I'd always been so careful, so consise in my actions all my life. This was a complete departure from everything I'd known.

What did I really know, though? I'd trusted Derek, and look where that had gotten me. Lied to and betrayed, after giving twenty-five years of myself to him. And I'd never had a clue. I'd never even suspected. So maybe the amount of time you knew wasn't a good indicator of who was trustworthy and who wasn't. I didn't feel, at least after I'd pepper sprayed him, that Logan was untrustworthy.

Well, I'd given my word. I needed to live up to it.

Logan drove off the ferry, and I looked up Tethys on my phone. She was supposedly one of the Titans, and a goddess of fresh water, but I guessed that could stretch and might include the sea. After all, fresh water ran to the sea. Why had she contacted me? What did it mean? I closed out my browser. One thing at a time, or my head might explode.

"What can I expect when we go and visit your client?" I asked, focusing on the task at hand. "What part do you expect me to play?"

"I think maybe not say anything, and let me introduce you as a colleague, if I have to introduce you at all. Not the Oracle. No way. If he hasn't sought you out, he has no need of you. I don't want to put you in danger."

"Kind of too late for that," I said. "I'm off for a day trip with a man who may or may not be a thief of the magical variety. I have a new job, so to speak, and I don't know enough about it, in my opinion. So maybe worrying about danger is not really on the list of concerns here."

"That doesn't mean I won't fight to keep you safe," he said as we pulled off the ferry. I could hear the sincerity in his words. "Which brings me to something else. Do you have a guest house, or somewhere in the basement, or something, where I can stay?"

"You want to stay at my house?" I didn't know how I felt about that.

Logan nodded. "I know it sounds like I'm falling into creeper territory, but I feel like I need to. I don't have a good reason, I can't give you proof or anything. It's just a feeling, and that, more than anything else, has kept me alive the past seven years."

I considered his words. Rolled them over in my mind, testing them for sincerity. I didn't feel anything that felt... off. "Okay. I have somewhere you can stay."

"Good. I'll feel better if I'm able to make sure you're safe while we're working together."

"Is that normal?" I asked.

"I don't know. I'm probably not the best person to ask," Logan said apologetically. "Maybe your spirit friend?"

"Oh, yeah, right," I said. Another question for Florry. I'd have to make time for her tonight as well. She was like an older version of Shelly. Both of whom could make my life miserable. Well, after a fashion, I thought with a grin.

"Do you have any magic?" Logan asked.

"What?"

"Magic. Do you have any?"

"Not that I know of. But apparently, it will show up, one way or another."

"That's all you got?" Logan asked, looking over with a frown. "Nothing more than that?"

"You're not the only one who gets unclear messages via your feelings," I said, gazing out the window.

Logan made a choking sound, and I realized he was laughing. "And I thought I had it bad being dropped in the desert," he said.

"Well, I'm not quite in the desert, but I am reminded daily of all the things I don't know."

"It will come," Logan said reassuringly. "I know it doesn't seem like it, but it will."

"I hope so," I said. There was no point in telling him that once I made it through this, I was going to try and rid myself of being the Oracle.

Or was I? I'd been sure about this decision two days ago and now? I wasn't so sure.

I hated indecision.

"Okay, we're here. He's not going to be happy to see me, since our business has been concluded. Stay next to me, and let me do the talking. Although you could look stern, or disapproving." Logan glanced at me.

I laughed. "All right, but I'm going to demand some lunch when this is over. I didn't have much for breakfast."

He pulled into a narrow driveway next to a tall brownstone. It looked old, and like it needed a good power wash.

I followed Logan out, walking next to him. We walked up the stairs and I put my hands behind my back as Logan rang the doorbell. I didn't want to fidget. It wouldn't help the image I was supposed to be projecting.

Logan rang the bell again.

There were footsteps and then a man pulled the door open. Horror and surprise mingled on his face. "What are you doing here?" he hissed.

"Peter, I find that we have further business." Logan was cool.

"No, we don't," Peter said.

"We can talk about it inside, in private, or out here where anyone could listen in," Logan said.

The two of them glared at one another, the tension so thick I could practically touch it.

Then Peter's shoulder's sagged, his eyes sliding to the left and right as he peered up and down the street. "Fine, come in. But you're not staying long."

Logan walked in without a word. I followed, nearly stepping on the heels of his shoes. I didn't like how this felt. Not at all. Talking about danger was one thing; heading straight into it was another.

Peter veered to the left, pushing open a door into what looked to be a study. "This is far enough," he snarled.

I stopped when Logan did.

"What do you want?" Peter whipped around, his eyes wild and angry.

"Who did you think I was when we met?" Logan asked.

"What?" Peter asked, his anger fading a tiny bit.

"You called me something else when we first met. Who did you think I was?" Logan's question was calm.

Peter's eyes bugged out. "Are you kidding me?"

"Do I look like I'm kidding?" Logan asked.

Peter stood still, and I could see the wheels of his brain turning. He was weighing how much to say.

"You don't remember?" he asked, and there was a sly tone to his question.

"No, I do not," Logan said. "Which is no matter. While I might have lost some of my memories, I am perfectly capable of dealing with betrayal." The last word came out in a growl.

Peter's face visibly paled. "Yes, yes, I can see that. Fine, fine. We met once before, maybe ten years ago? I don't remember. But your name wasn't Logan, then."

"How did we meet?" Logan asked.

Peter didn't respond, and a calculating expression came over his face.

Without knowing what I was doing, I stepped out in front of Logan. "You would do well to tell us the truth," I said, not recognizing my own voice. "Choose your next words carefully, Mr. Dunleavy."

I felt Logan's hand on my arm, but I ignored it, not taking my eyes off Peter.

He took a couple of steps backwards, his hands up. "All right, all right, all right. Your name was Caleb Montgomery. We did a deal, for something a lot more dangerous than our recent business."

"What was the deal for?" Logan asked.

"Is that really necessary?" Peter asked. "It was over ten years ago. No matter to you now."

"Answer the question, Mr. Dunleavy," I said.

His shoulders sagged, this time in defeat. "We did business for a compelling ring. It was a large platinum ring, imbued with fae magic."

"There are fae?" I whispered to Logan.

"Later," he said out of the side of his mouth. "How much did that cost you?" he asked Peter Dunleavy.

"A lot. A very great sum. But I had to have it," Peter said.

"Have you used it?" Logan asked.

"That is definitely none of your business. You know better than to ask that of any collectors you work with, Montgomery, or Gentry, or whatever your name is. I've answered your questions. Now get out." Peter seemed to have found his spine.

I waited, wanting to see what Logan would do.

Logan said, "Thank you for your time. I appreciate it." He smiled, but it wasn't pleasant. It was the smile of a predator about to eat his prey. Then he turned, saying to me easily, "I think it's time for us to go."

As we walked out of the study, and out the front door, I didn't speak. I waited until we were on the sidewalk to say, "Thank you for not saying my name in there."

"What?" Logan jumped at my words. "Sorry, I was lost in thought."

"Oh, okay," I said. "But thank you for not saying my name."

"I didn't want him to know anything about you," he said.

"Well, it's obvious I'm your friend, or at least your ally," I said.

"Is that such a bad thing?" Logan asked as we got in the car.

"I don't think so, but I haven't known you long," I said. "At least we have a name that we can look up."

"Caleb Montgomery is pretty basic," Logan said.

"Yes, but a name and maybe a picture of you?"

He shook his head. "I have put my own picture in search engines hundreds of times. Nothing comes up."

"Well, aren't you positive and optimistic," I rolled my eyes.

"I stopped getting my hope up a long time ago," Logan said.

"Did you ever have a name to go on before?" I asked.

"No," he admitted. "Okay, that might not be such a bad thing."

"Why don't we wait and see before we go all doom and gloom?"

"If you insist," his tone was mocking.

"I do. Now what's for lunch? I'm starving."

"Do you have a preference?" Logan asked.

I came to New Bedford regularly to shop, so I directed him to a burger place I liked. We sat at a table in the corner and ate until I felt like I couldn't move. "That was delicious," I said. "I haven't eaten that much in ages."

"Fries are hard to resist," Logan teased.

"Indeed. So are you going to tell me what you brought along as insurance?"

His eyebrows went up. He didn't speak.

Neither did I. I merely waited.

"Fine. I brought a charismatic," he said.

"What is that?"

"It's an object that has a spell on it to compel the person you give it to. It makes them more amenable to your request."

"You seem to deal an awful lot in shady things," I said. "Speaking of which, let's look up Caleb." I pulled out my phone and started to look up all sorts of combinations of Caleb Montgomery. Logan was right, it was a common name.

"None of these is you," I said in disgust a while later.

He shrugged. "I figured it was a fake name."

"Do you think Peter lied to you?"

"No," Logan shook his head. "I just felt sure I was using a false name."

"What were you doing that you used a false name?" I asked. I should be worried. I should. But I wasn't. Was that a good or bad thing?

"Probably something similar to what I'm doing now, if I helped him get a compulsion ring."

"Is that the same thing as a charismatic?"

"No," Logan said, leaning forward and lowering his voice. "A charismatic is a one-time use kind of thing.

Had I used it today, it would just be a rock once it was done. It's just any item with a spell attached. A compulsion ring is a magical item that has a power all its own. The wearer can compel those around him."

"And it was fae magic?" I lowered my voice also.

He nodded. "Yes. It was—is—a rare item. The fae tend to keep their magical items to themselves. He must have paid a lot for it."

I sat back, thinking. "You know, if you were doing this before, and working for people who paid a lot of money, you have to have had a bank account."

His eyes widened. "I didn't even think about that."

"Well, do you have one now? I mean, do you stuff your money under a mattress?"

"Of course I have bank accounts. Who stuffs money under mattresses?"

"Exactly," I said. "Maybe if we could find a bank account traceable to Caleb Montgomery, we can track that backwards to your real name."

"I wish we'd thought of this before," Logan said.

"I think I was too nervous," I admitted. "I'm sorry."

"That's not on you," Logan said. "Let me call him." He pulled out his phone. "Peter," he said.

I could hear the angry tones of Peter Dunleavy from where I sat.

"This is the last thing I need from you. I would like a record of any bank transactions from the sale of the ring," Logan said calmly. Then he listened. "Yes. That's exactly it." More silence, in which I could hear Peter continuing to talk angrily. "Yes, I would be willing to give you my word that I won't contact you again."

He nodded, listening. "Yes, please use the contact info you used before. Thank you, Peter." He ended the call.

"This is good, right?" I asked.

"We'll see. But it's something I haven't thought about before."

"I feel stupid not thinking about this earlier," I said.

"I've been thinking about this for seven years, and I didn't think about it. I think I'm used to expecting to find nothing," Logan said.

"Well, now we have something."

"That depends on what Peter sends me," Logan replied.

"Well, wait to see if you need to be disappointed. Now, I need to get back. I have some things to take care of tonight." I wanted to get home. I felt exposed being here, having come out with Logan.

But this was my job, wasn't it? To help those who came to me? Not only did I need to talk with Florry, I needed to get the grimoire to reveal more to me. Which had only happened as I was leafing through the blank pages, thinking about what I wanted to know.

The ferry ride back to Martha's Vineyard was uneventful. Logan drove us back to my house. "If you want, you can get settled now. I have an extra room," I said.

"That would be great," Logan said. "I've been staying at one of the local inns. But something tells me I need to be here."

I nodded. My home was in the older section of Oak Bluffs, originally an old Methodist campground. The houses were built in the 1800s to handle the campers, and now, there were still hundreds of them in our little town. I was fortunate. I had one of the larger homes, with what was technically four bedrooms. One of them was large enough to hold only a bed and a desk, which had worked well when Theo and Kris were ready to stop sharing a room. When the kids stayed over now, the boys preferred to share a room once more, and I'd turned the small bedroom into a guest room.

Oh, hell. The kids were expected this weekend. I might have to ask Logan to leave. Well, I'd deal with that when the time came. I had a couple of days. "I'll show you the room, and then you can move your things over. I need to do some work."

"Of course," Logan said. "I appreciate you being willing to come out with me, be hands on, as it were."

"Well, you could be getting lucky that you're my first client," I said.

"I'll take it," he laughed. "While you're working, I'll see what I can find out with the bank information Peter is supposed to send."

"Okay," I said. "Come on in, and I'll show you the room."

We walked into the house together, and I tried not to think about my neighbors peering out their windows. I took him upstairs and showed him the room and the bathroom that was a short distance down the hall.

"I can take it from here. I'll ring the bell when I come back," Logan said.

"All right," I said, and with a glance over my shoulder, I walked to the master suite. I shut the door, and leaned against it. The weight of the day hit me—the encounter with Peter Dunleavy, the whisperings of Tethys, and all the stuff I needed to ask Florry. But first, I took the grimoire out of my scarf drawer where I'd hidden it, and thumbed through the pages. No writing appeared.

"Isn't there some kind of how-to section?" I grumbled. "Can't I get a break?"

"Not really," Florry's voice replied.

I looked around to see her standing near the window. "No one else can see you, can they?" I asked.

"Nope. Just you, toots. I got a sense we needed to talk."

"You think?" I asked. "God, I don't even know where to begin."

"What did you and shifter boy agree to in terms of compensation?" Florry asked.

"Service, like you suggested," I said. "You were there. We didn't agree on anything more specific."

"That's a good thing. He might be your companion." Florry was thoughtful.

"My what?"

"I had a friend, someone that I met during my first year as the Oracle. Her name was Caro, and she was the complete opposite of me. German, prim, proper, and the best damn researcher I'd ever met. We hit it off, and she ended up moving to Lost Cause, so she could help me. It's a thing with us, with the Oracles. We often have humans who end up being besties. Caro was the best, truest friend I ever had. That's the word you kids are using, right?" Florry grinned. "Logan might be your bestie."

"I don't know about that," I said. "I think I just don't know what the hell I'm doing." The thought of seeing him regularly, daily—I wasn't sure I could handle that right now. It brought up too many emotions. And other things.

"I think you're doing fine. The more you do this, the more your instincts, your feelings, your intuition, and your dreams will guide you. But you're following your dreams—"

"Which have nothing to do with this case!" I threw up my hands. It was frustrating, dreaming of the same party over and over. "I think I have to help the man in the dream before I can help Logan."

"Then you need to go with that."

"I have no idea who the man in the dream is," I fumed.

"Be patient. That's a key thing to learn. You get more information as time goes on."

"Heaven help anyone who has a life or death concern."

"They're all life and death concerns, to the consultants," Florry replied. "But this can't be rushed."

"I heard from someone named Tethys today," I said, changing the subject.

Florry's eyebrows went up toward her flyaway hair. "Really? Why? What did she want?"

I laughed. "She told me more of what you're selling. I have to be patient, the sea will reveal things when it's ready to, all women are of the sea." I waved. "That sort of thing."

"I never heard from her," Florry said.

"You know who she is?" I asked.

"Of course. Did you?"

I shook my head. "No, I looked her up while I was on the ferry today. But why would she contact me?"

Florry shrugged. "You should just plan on hearing from lots of folks now that you're the Oracle. It comes with the job."

"What about magic? When does that come with the job? I want to be able to defend myself. I don't want people to be able to pop into my head whenever they feel like it."

"Tethys is kind of a special case. She's a goddess, an old goddess. She does what she wants. Besides, don't you have a mean pepper spray and Taser game?" Florry asked, grinning.

"Yes, but what is that going to do for me against some magical person who can knock me on my butt?" I retorted.

"It's better than nothing. I don't know, to answer your question. I got really good at a binding spell, which would let me stop people in their tracks. Read the grimoire. Because you're part of this world now, you have options. Whatever your specific skill is, it will show itself."

"What does that mean? What does any of this mean? And what if I don't want to continue?" I asked, thinking of my musings earlier today. "Also, the grimoire is being very choosy about what it shows me."

"Well, you don't get much of a choice until you succeed or fail with your first consultant. You might talk to Goldie, as well."

"He's been pretty quiet today," I said. It was annoying.

"He's like that," Florry said. "He's getting to know you. Once he knows you better, he won't shut up."

"Can I see the other Oracles?" I asked.

"No. Just me. That's the deal. I'm your lifeline." She laughed.

"How long do we live?" I asked.

"Well, that depends. I was eighty-six when I died. At least, that's how old I think I was. Time is strange when you're the Oracle." Her eyes were distant.

"That doesn't really answer my question."

"I know," Florry said. "It's not meant to." She looked at me then, fully present now. "You'll live as long as you're supposed to. Don't borrow trouble. What else?"

"What service should I ask Logan for? You know, for payment?"

"You have things that need doing around the house? Heavy lifting, projects? You want to have him accompany you when you travel? You can ask him."

"How long is this service obligation for?"

"You negotiate that with him. Ask him what he's willing to give. I'd wait a bit, though. See how far you get on his case."

"Again, not really an answer."

"Being the Oracle kind of rubs off on you," Florry said. "You'll get better at vague answers. What are you going to do about your kids?"

"What do you mean?" I was on the defensive immediately.

"You have to tell them something," she said.

"Maybe I'll tell them I have a new hobby, and that it's no big deal."

"That's actually not bad," Florry said. "Covers a lot. Gets you off the hook. You can't tell 'em," she added.

"I wasn't planning to."

"It can put them in danger."

"Oh, the more you tell me, the more this is sounding so appealing." I got up. I wanted to take a shower, and then start getting ready for Shelly's coming over.

"Oh, hell," I said.

"What?"

"What in the world am I going to tell Shelly about Logan?"

Florry's laughter followed me into the bathroom. I could hear her chuckling even after I shut the door hard.

CHAPTER TEN

I was busy in the kitchen putting together the fixings for salad when the doorbell rang. It was Logan, a duffle bag in hand and a backpack on his shoulder. "Come in," I said.

He walked right up the stairs, and I could hear him moving around in the small guest room. I'd been thinking about what Florry had said, that there were often companions for the Oracle. But he wasn't human, and she'd specifically said human. Logan was a shifter. He had his own life.

And he was too darn attractive. I couldn't ignore that, even as much as I wanted to.

Thudding on the steps told me he was coming downstairs. I'd decided that I'd introduce him to Shelly as a friend of Derek's, who had come to pay his respects, and leave it there. Shelly would take that information to all sorts of new heights all by herself.

"What are you making? Can I help you?" Logan asked as he came into the kitchen.

"I have a friend coming over. She's bringing dinner. I'm just making salad, and toasting some bread." I kept garlic bread at the ready, as it was one of my favorite comfort foods. Which Shelly knew.

"And you want me out of the way?" Logan asked knowingly.

"This is my best friend," I sighed. "It's going to be hard enough to keep the whole Oracle thing from her. Now I have to tell her something about you."

"How long have you been friends?" Logan asked.

"Over twenty years," I said.

"Then just tell her the truth," he shrugged.

"What? Tell her the whole ancient Oracle thing, the fact I have an old lady as a spiritual guide, that you're a consultant, that I might have magic skill popping up at some point? That I have a magical armband disguised as a tattoo? And the armband talks?" I threw my hands up. "She's likely to commit me."

"Or not," Logan said. "Good friends are usually pretty forgiving."

"I don't want to put her in danger," I said.

"You're not responsible for what other people might do. People who know you could be in danger whether you told them you're the Oracle or not," he argued.

"I'll think about it," I said. I liked the idea of telling the truth, because I hated lying, and it would be nice to have one person in my regular life who knew the truth. The entire truth.

"I'll be whoever you want to introduce me as," Logan said. "Whatever you want. I can go and grab dinner out, if that makes things easier."

"No, don't do that," I said. "She'll bring too much. She always does. But maybe head upstairs before she gets here, so I have a chance to tell her everything. Hey, speaking of which, what did you find out about the bank account?"

He sat down in one of the chairs at the island. "Well, it's a Swiss bank account, which means it's locked down tighter than Fort Knox. I'm going to have to hire someone to see if they can crack it, and at least get me a name. They can't release any info legally from the bank without the account owner's permission, which I can't give." He sighed. "They're great for hiding your money, but they suck when you need to find out anything."

"It's a start," I said.

"It is, and it's more than I had before, so thank you," Logan inclined his head formally. "I've discovered more since I came to see you than I have in seven years. I'm going to head upstairs, make some phone calls. When you're ready for me to come down, just say so."

"What do you mean?" I asked.

"I'm a shifter, remember? I have exceptional hearing. I'll hear you."

"Well, okay," I said as he walked upstairs. The idea made me a little uncomfortable. He heard everything?

Great.

When the doorbell rang again—my life was becoming defined by my visitors—I still hadn't fully made up my mind what I would share. Shelly came in carrying a casserole dish and gave me a big, one-armed hug.

"Hey," she said. "Whose car is in your driveway? I hope you're in the mood for baked ziti," she gestured with the casserole dish.

Well. Decision made. "Come in, and let me tell you all about it."

"Oh, ho!" Shelly hooted. "Is this about Mr. Wrong at the wrong time?"

"Not at all, although he's part of what I want to tell you about."

"I can't wait," Shelly said gleefully.

Forty-five minutes later, she sat across from me on the couch, rubbing her hands together and looking off in the distance.

"Shell, say something," I said, trying not to beg.

She blinked, and looked at me. "That was totally not what I expected to hear, Wynter. Not at all. Let me see the armband."

I got up and sat next to her, holding out my right arm.

She traced the serpent with her forefinger, not speaking.

Easy, I heard Goldie's voice.

"Shush," I said.

"I didn't say anything," Shelly said.

"I know. He did," I pointed at my arm.

"It talks to you? Oh, that's right. You said that," Shelly said, almost to herself. "Then why the heck aren't you being more helpful, Snaky poo?"

That's not how this works, Goldie said, his tone stiff. *Finding her way is part of the Oracle's journey.*

I laughed out loud as I relayed his words to Shelly.

"Hogwash," she said. "If you're supposed to be the helper, then you actually need to help. This isn't a difficult concept, Snaky."

If she must call me something, it's Goldie, Goldie said. He sounded aggrieved.

Which made me laugh more. It had been the right thing to tell Shelly. I relayed his words once more.

"Nope. You're Snaky to me. Until you stop being a snake in the grass, and really help my friend." Shelly shook her head. "Well, let's eat. And call down your... what do you call him?" She got up from the couch, patting my thigh as she did so.

"Consultant. That's what those looking for help are called. Consultants."

"Well, get him down here. I want to see him for myself. We have plenty of food."

"Logan," I said out loud.

A moment later, he bounded down the steps. As he came into the kitchen, I heard Shelly's intake of breath.

"I'm not interrupting, am I?" Logan asked, a smile on his face.

"Holy Joseph," Shelly breathed. "Wynter, he can come over and stay at my place and be a consultant any time."

"I'm right here. Should I feel objectified?" Logan asked.

"If you want. Yes, please," Shelly replied. She visibly eyed him up and down.

"Oh, for Pete's sake," I said.

"Wynter, you didn't tell me he was…" Shelly began.

"Was what?" I asked, feeling annoyed.

"All this," Shelly waved a hand up and down Logan's physique.

"I one hundred percent feel objectified," Logan said. He was trying not to laugh.

"Oh, hush," Shelly said. "A man who looks like you do should expect it now and then. And we're all friends here, so as an old lady who is your friend, and absolutely no danger to your virtue," she winked at Logan, "I'm sure you'll allow me some grace."

He gave up then, and laughed loudly. His laugh was rich and full, and Shelly and I joined in.

"We're going to get along fine, big man," Shelly said.

"What will your husband say?" Logan teased.

"Not a darn thing," she replied. "The only one alive is an ex, and I don't give a fig what he says."

Dinner was full of laughter and teasing. I'd made the right decision to tell Shelly, and for the first time since this whole thing had begun, I felt better.

"Thank you," I said, hugging my friend as she got ready to leave. "Thanks for not having me committed."

"I've always known there was magic in the world, Wyn," she said, kissing my cheek. "I just never thought I'd get to see it. And now I do. So thank you for trusting me. I'm here for whatever you need. Are you going to tell the kids?"

I shook my head. "No. They're coming over on Saturday to discuss how to deal with Natalie and her kids."

"I think not telling them about this new wrinkle in your life is for the best. Your kids are pretty accepting, but with Derek passing, they might think you've lost the plot and need to get carted off to the home." Shelly's favorite insult was that whatever it was I'd done was going to get me carted off to the old folks' home. Given that she was ten years older, I rather thought it was one of her fears, but it had become a joke between us.

"Anything but that," I said.

"Exactly. Call me this week, let me know you're okay. And you can send Logan over to my place on Saturday. I'll keep him entertained."

With more laughter, I saw her out, and then went into the kitchen to finish cleaning up.

Logan was loading dishes into the dishwasher. "Was that better than you expected?"

"It was," I said. "But now she's going to make all sorts of demands on you, so just know you brought some of this on yourself."

"That's all right," Logan said with a laugh. "She'll probably feed me when I go over on Saturday."

"Oh, you heard that? You don't have to, if you have other things to do," I said.

"Shifter, remember?" He tapped his ear. "It's all right. I don't mind making things easier for you. I like her," he said.

"I'm glad I told her," I said.

"It's good to have an ally in your daily life," he said. "Having to hide who you are is tough."

I nodded, thinking that he knew what he was talking about. After we were done in the kitchen, I yawned. "I'm going to bed. It's been a long day."

"Night, Wynter," he said.

"Good night." I left him in the living room, and checked the doors before I went upstairs. Everything was locked. Once in my room, I made sure that my pepper spray and Taser were within reach. Then I got into my pajamas, and gratefully crawled into bed. It had been a long day. My eyes closed, and I drifted off to sleep.

When my eyes opened, the room was dark, and the house was silent in the manner of a house in the middle of the night. I lay still, listening. My heart was racing, and I could tell that something was not right.

Get up, Goldie said.

"What?" My voice came out as a croak.

Don't speak. I'll hear your thoughts. Get up. Now. His voice brooked no argument.

What's wrong? I threw back the blankets as my feet felt around for my slippers on the floor.

And then I realized that while I was sitting up in bed, I was also lying down still, asleep.

What the hell? I thought.

Your physical form will be safe. It's your astral form we need to protect. Get up, and find the shadows, Goldie said.

Being astral didn't feel any different than if I'd gotten my body out of bed. I looked around the room, and went toward my closet. As I reached for the handle, Goldie spoke again.

No. Just walk through. You need to be in the deepest corner, and stay very still.

I would have probably taken a moment to freak out if I didn't hear the worry in Goldie's words. I walked through the door of the closet, which felt weird as hell, and went to where my clothes were hanging. I walked through them as well, stopping when I reached the wall.

What's going on? I thought.

Ariadne and her damn bull, Goldie said.

What?

Shut up, he said.

I heard it then. A dragging, like someone who was schlepping along, dragging their feet. A heavy breathing. A bull, Goldie had said. There was a bull in my house?

The dragging sounds, accompanied by heavy footfalls, got closer.

Then I heard a woman's voice, although I couldn't tell what she said.

Be very still, Goldie said.

I held my breath.

The steps were in my room, walking toward the bathroom. That meant they would go right past where I was hiding in the closet.

Then there was another set of footsteps. A hiss, and then a squeal. Then a loud snarl, and a roar, and the floor shook out in front of the closet. It sounded like someone had dropped a Mack truck right outside the door.

The door shuddered as the Mack truck, or bull, or whatever, hit it. But it didn't open. I must have breathed, but I didn't think so. I was pressed against the wall of my closet, and I hadn't felt myself move, much less breathe. I was too scared.

There was a screeching sound, like nails on a chalkboard, against the wall next to the closet, and then another hiss. A thud, and then a roar, and then things were quiet.

Wynter, stay with me, I heard Goldie's voice, but it seemed like it was a long way away. *I need you to get back to your body.*

I'm so tired, I thought.

I know. I think he's gone.

The door to the closet opened, and my entire form tensed.

"Wynter?" It was Logan. "I know you're in your bed, but you're not all there. Where are you?"

Back to your body, Goldie said firmly.

With great effort, I pushed myself out of the closet, feeling my eyes fighting to close. I moved past Logan, who wasn't wearing a shirt and back toward my bed. My body was still in the bed, for all the world sleeping peacefully. I sat down on the bed, and let my form sink down, barely aware of what I was doing.

Then my eyes were wide open and I was sitting up in bed—me, all of me, body and mind, my heart racing and my fingers shaking. "What was that?" I asked. Then I looked at Logan. He was missing a shirt, and apparently everything else, as well. The bottom half of him was wrapped in my mother's quilt that usually lived at the foot of my bed. "Why are you wearing my quilt?"

"That was a bull, and I was just going to ask you why it was in your room, hunting."

"How do you know it was hunting?" I pulled the sheets up to my chest, feeling even more frightened.

"I knew," Logan smiled. "As to why I'm wearing a quilt —well, I don't wear anything when I shift. I thought you might prefer this to me being naked."

My cheeks went hot, and my eyes slid away from his very bare, very nicely formed chest. "You're right. I appreciate your consideration. Why was a bull in here hunting me?" I stopped. "Goldie!" I shouted.

"Why are you shouting for Goldie?" Logan asked, looking around.

"Because he woke me up, told me to get up."

"You astral projected? Without even thinking about it?"

"I guess," I said. "I woke up knowing that something was wrong, and then he told me to get up and hide in the shadows. Was that thing real?" I asked.

Logan rotated one arm, his hand rubbing at his shoulder. "Yes. At least, the bruise that's forming on my shoulder says the bull was real."

"What did it want?"

"You? What else is there?" Logan asked, as though this was understood.

"Goldie," I said again. "Answers."

That was the Minotaur, from Greek legend. He is long dead, but he travels with Ariadne, his sister. She was abandoned by Theseus after he killed the Minotaur on Crete. She eventually married Dionysius, but she always wanted to be one of the priestesses at Delphi. She was never accepted. Once she died, her desire took on a new form. When there's a new Oracle, and the Oracle hasn't solved the request of their first consultant, the Oracle is... vulnerable. I can be taken, which means the Oracle would pass to whomever took it. She wants the armband, wants to be the Oracle.

I relayed all this to Logan, whose face darkened as I kept speaking. I stopped, and said, "Goldie, you couldn't have told me this before? Really?"

I hoped you would answer Logan's questions before she found you.

"Well, that didn't work!" I flared.

"No, it did not. Is she going to try again?" Logan asked, his voice low and dangerous.

Probably, Goldie said. He sounded tired.

I relayed his answer to Logan.

"Then we have to solve this," Logan said. "The damn armband is sure she can't come after you once you are officially the Oracle, like forever and ever?"

Once the first consultant has been answered, there is no question as to who is the Oracle, Goldie said.

"Nothing about this—this—Adriane—"

"Ariadne," Logan said.

"Be quiet," I snapped. "Nothing about her or the bull is in the grimoire! At least, nothing that I've been shown. You didn't tell me a thing! Neither did Florry! What the hell?" I yelled. "Are you trying to get me killed? I can't solve a thing if I'm dead!"

"They should have told you," Logan said. He was furious. "How long before they try again?"

I don't know, Goldie said.

"I'm going to shift, and spend the night in here," Logan said. "In case they come back."

I didn't say anything. I was shaking, not only from fear, but from anger. This had suddenly taken another turn, and one that was far more dangerous. I should have been told. *You should have told me*, I thought.

Would it have helped? There was a chance she wouldn't find you, Goldie said. *I had to take that chance. If you were scared, you wouldn't have done as well as you've been doing.*

I haven't been doing well at all. I shook my head.

Nonsense, my snake armband said. *You've managed to dream, to find the grimoire, to make contact with Florry, to dream about your consultant, to project your spirit from your body, to figure out how to begin to direct your visions with the flames. You've done extremely well.*

You're just saying that because I nearly died. I glared at my arm.

No, I am not. I do not offer shallow praise.

You don't offer much at all, I thought, frowning.

I cannot afford to become attached until I know that we shall be together, Goldie said. *You must solve Logan's mystery. Only then will you be safe.*

Great. That's completely reassuring, I thought.

"Are you all right?" Logan asked.

"I'm as fine as I can be. Just arguing with my armband," I said crossly. Which sounded so ridiculous I started to laugh.

Logan looked at me like I'd lost my mind, but I couldn't help it. It was probably stress, but I kept laughing, and eventually, he laughed with me. When whatever it was had worked itself out, I got out of bed —for real this time, and slid my feet into my slippers. "I'm going to wash my face, and then go get a drink of water, and try to go back to sleep," I said. "Do you need anything from downstairs?"

"Let me go put on some pants. I want to make sure nothing is downstairs waiting for you," Logan said.

While he went to go get decent, I washed my face, and ran my hands through my hair. In less than two minutes, Logan was back in my room, wearing black gym pants, gathered at the ankle. He'd put on a shirt as well, which was a good thing. It was hard to avoid staring at his well-defined chest. He also had folded up the quilt, and laid it on the footboard. "Thanks for the loan," he grinned.

"Of course," I said. "Let's go see if there's anyone else in my house." Now that the fear was moving away, I was mad. Damn it. Why did anyone think they had a right to be in my house? To take away something that had come to me? It didn't matter that I might not want to keep it. For right now, it was mine.

Logan moved in front of me and made his way down the stairs. The house was quiet. Normally, that didn't bother me, but now, it felt eerie. Like there was someone or something waiting for me in the shadows.

I stopped in the kitchen as Logan prowled through the rest of the main floor. I was drinking a glass of water when he came back into the kitchen.

"There's no one here, and all the doors are locked."

"So they got in by magic," I said. "That kind of freaks me out, Logan."

"Understandable. But they won't try again tonight, so you can go back to sleep. I'll shift, and sleep in your room just to be sure."

"Okay," I said. "I need to help you find your past. That's the only way I'm going to get rid of this." I thought some more about what I'd heard. "Could you see the minotaur?"

Logan nodded. "I could. And he was real. I jumped on him, bit him on the shoulder. He tasted real. Real nasty," he made a face. "Then he hit my shoulder to toss me off. I tried to get hold of him again, but he disappeared."

"Did you see a woman?" I asked, remembering hearing a feminine voice.

"No. Why? Did you?"

"I thought I heard her," I said, wondering if I was imagining things. "It must have been Ariadne, or her ghost, or something. Who else would hang around with the minotaur?"

"I don't know," Logan said. "You think you can get back to sleep?"

"I'm going to try," I said.

We walked back upstairs.

"I'll be back. Don't scream when you see me," Logan warned. His green eyes looked golden in the dim light of the hall.

"I won't."

He walked into the guest room. I stood at my door, arms tightly folded across my chest. There was no noise, no hint of what was going on in my guest room, and then a sleek, powerful, dark shadow came padding out from where Logan had entered.

I knew, in my head, that I was going to see a big cat come out, but the reality of it didn't work quite as smoothly in my brain.

He was beautiful. Dangerous and scary, too. But absolutely beautiful. It nearly took my breath away.

"Well, let's go," I said, and I walked into my room.

The panther followed. He walked around the room, then down the small hall with the closets and into the bathroom. I could hear the click of his nails against the tile floor. He appeared in the hallway, and came back to where I stood. His large head butted against my leg, My hand came down of its own accord and rubbed the top of his head.

The panther looked up at me, his expression making it clear what he thought of such an action.

"I'm sorry," I said. "Habit."

The panther blinked, and moved toward the corner. He turned in a small circle once, then twice, and curled up. His head rested on his paws, and his golden eyes were watchful.

I got into bed, wary of the panther watching my every move. It was disconcerting. If I was honest, it made me feel like a rabbit. One who couldn't get away. After everything that had happened, I was sure I wouldn't be able to sleep, but my eyes closed as my head hit the pillow, and I knew no more.

CHAPTER ELEVEN

The next morning when my eyes opened, I looked toward the corner where Logan the panther had been staring at me. It was empty. I had to admit, I was relieved. Trying to get myself together with those golden eyes watching me might have been the end of me. At least, I might have peed my pants in fear.

Logan the panther was scary.

I showered and got ready for the day. I had to do some shopping, both for Logan and myself since he was here, and for the kids coming this weekend. They'd probably stay the night as they had before when I'd told them the truth about Derek.

Logan was in front of the stove when I came down-stairs, and it smelled delicious. I wasn't used to anyone cooking for me. But Shelly had brought dinner last night, and now breakfast.

I could get used to someone else doing the cooking, I thought.

"How did you sleep?" Logan didn't turn around.

"Better than I expected. I need to go out today, do some shopping. And I need to talk to Florry."

"Florry?"

"Spirit guide," I waved a hand. "What's on your agenda?"

"I have to go through my files of my equally nefarious colleagues and see who can break into a Swiss account," he said, grinning. He put a plate of bacon, sliced avocados and tomatoes, and Toad in the Hole in front of me. "I love this," I said. "My gran used to make Toad in the Hole."

"Mark, my closest friend, loves it. This is his favorite breakfast. I find that I make it more than any other, so it must be mine, too," Logan said.

Once we finished, I offered to clean up. Logan was out of the kitchen before I could say another word. I loaded the dishwasher and wiped down the counters, and then made my grocery list.

With everything that had been going on, it was kind of nice to do something normal. Mundane. That didn't carry a threat of death.

I pulled into the parking lot at the grocery store, and walked in, feeling better. I started on my list, and moved through the store faster than normal. It was as I was working through the produce part of my list that I noticed the group of three women who were staring at me.

One of them was Hazel Babbington, the owner of the Oak Bluffs Inn. She met my eyes, and then nodded, and turned to her friends.

They weren't even trying to hide it.

I lifted my chin, and started bagging cucumbers.

"Mrs. Chastain," I heard next to me on my right.

I was expecting one of the gossipy women, but this was a man. He was tall, very sleek and polished, his blond hair slicked back. He wore a black tee shirt and jeans, and outside of being darkly handsome, didn't stand out.

But he radiated menace. I could feel it even though he was at least three feet away from me.

"May I help you?" I asked, my tone as frosty as I could manage.

"I believe you can," the man said, leaning forward, pretending to look at the red peppers. "You have something we want, and you were not supposed to get it." His gaze turned to me, down to my arm. He focused on Goldie like a laser. "That is not yours."

"Oh, I think it is," I said. First a Greek myth and her pet bull brother, and now this shady character with the vibe of a bad movie villain? While I wasn't sure I wanted to be the Oracle forever and ever, there sure were a lot of people who did want it.

Which was something to consider. Both good, that this could be good for me, and bad, because people would try to kill me.

Only until I solved my first request. Then the Oracle wasn't in doubt. I guess I was a whole lot of doubt to those watching right now.

"It chose me," I said, giving him eyeball for eyeball. "While I didn't choose this, I accept that I've been chosen, and it's not on you or anyone else to say otherwise."

"I disagree, Mrs. Chastain. You have a very lovely tattoo, and it would make an even lovelier piece of jewelry, even if there was some difficulty," he glanced down again, a truly evil smile tilting the corners of his lips, "Removing it from its present resting place."

That was a Grade A serious threat. "That is not your decision to make," I said again.

"We can agree to disagree, Wynter," he said, drawing out my name in an unpleasant manner. "There is nothing wrong with disagreement. But you are not correct, and should you persist in your incorrect notions, we will be forced to correct them for you. Return that which is not yours, and all will be well. We'll even replace what you lost to Arizona." He smiled at me, all sweetness and light.

A cold shiver went through me, like when you jump in cold water on a hot day. It shook me to my core, making it impossible for me to move, to even speak. How did they know about Natalie? About the insurance money? Because it was obvious he knew.

"All you need to do is make the right choice. This isn't your world, isn't your fight. Just return the armband, and all this nasty business goes away."

"What did you do to Ash?" I finally managed to unfreeze my lips and speak.

"Mr. Flint is… fine," the blond man said, his eyes narrowing. Whatever he'd been expecting from me in the way of response after his many layered threats, this wasn't it. "He was a distraction. He should have never had the armband."

"Really? I got the distinct impression that not only was it his, but he'd been looking for it."

"The authorities meddle where they are not wanted all the time. That means nothing," the man said impatiently. "And their meddling does not concern our business, Mrs. Chastain."

I hated the way he said my name. It was interesting that he put Ash into the group of 'authorities', as he called it. What sort of authorities? Were there magical police?

Villain guy continued, "I know that you have obligations you must see through. But once you are done, call this number. If you choose not to," a small white card appeared between his forefinger and middle finger, "Then you cannot say you haven't been warned."

I took the card. "Thank you for letting me know," I said. I sounded calm, but my heartbeat was about to gallop out of my chest. I wished Logan was here.

I couldn't count on him, though. This was my fight, my burden, for the time being.

"It was a pleasure to meet you. I advise you to make the right choice while you still can, Mrs. Chastain. Good day." He inclined his head and walked away, whistling as though he hadn't a care in the world.

I couldn't move. This was the answer to my problems, right? Solve the current request before me, and then give up the Oracle. But to give it to that slimy guy? And whoever else was working with him? My entire being balked at the thought.

Looking down at the card, there was no name, no identifying information. Just a number.

Figures.

I tucked the card in my purse. With shaking hands, I picked up the bag that I'd started to put my cucumbers in when I felt someone else—several someone else's—come up on the other side of me.

"Well, Wynter, fancy seeing you here." It was Hazel Babbington, making her move. "Another man? That wasn't the Mr. Flint that disappeared from the Inn."

I turned to her. "No, it wasn't. My affairs are none of your business."

The two women behind Hazel, who I didn't know, both made noises of shock and offense.

"When you hurt my business at the Inn, yes indeed, missy, it is my business."

"I didn't do anything other than call the police when my friend went missing," I said. "What sort of Inn are you running, Hazel, that you don't have security? When Ash and I came in, there was no one at the desk. Anyone could come in, and they obviously did. If you're having business concerns, I'd venture a guess that it was based on potential guests not feeling that your establishment is safe."

Hazel gasped. "You hussy! How dare you?"

"You hateful old bat, I can ask you the same thing." I leaned closer, putting my face near hers. "If I were you, I'd be careful, Hazel. Gossip goes in all directions around here."

Her mouth opened and closed a few times, making her look like a fish gasping for air. Then she clamped it shut, glared at me, and stormed off, followed by her faithful companions, both of whom gave me some truly serious stink eye.

It was obviously the day for sideswiping me, so I finished up with my produce and hurried through the check out before anyone else could corner me. When I got home, I brought the groceries in, and collapsed on the couch. My hands were shaking, and I felt the way you did when you had gone too long without eating. Forcing myself up, I went to the fridge and drank orange juice right from the bottle, which I never did.

When my heartbeat calmed, I put away the groceries, and went back to the couch. "Florry," I called. "I really need your help."

She appeared, Olympia beer can in hand. "What?"

I told her about creepy blond guy at the store, and her face took on a serious expression.

"What is it about you, Wynter? I never had this many problems when I became the Oracle."

"You think this is my fault?" My outrage swelled.

She shrugged. "There's something about you that is drawing all of these beings to seek you out."

"Maybe because I don't know much of anything, and I'm weak, and all the people who are supposed to help aren't doing a thing?" My voice rose. "You also lived in the middle of a field in the middle of Kansas, Florry!"

"You're getting no better or worse what the rest of us got. You're going to have to figure it out," she said.

"How? I keep trying to ask to see how to help Logan, and all I keep getting is the party where I can't stop watching a group of people."

"Then you need to get into the party," Florry said, as though it were the most natural thing in the world. "Are you at the party? Or are you just watching? I didn't take you for the voyeur type," she added with a grin.

"Stop it," I said, before she decided to tease me. But I thought it over. I'd just been watching—observing, I amended, not wanting to see Florry's smirk. "You think that will make the difference?"

"You always see more clearly when you're involved in the action happening. You feel the emotions, you see the small things people are doing."

"I always thought you saw better from a distance, because you were able to see the bigger picture."

"Maybe," Florry said. "Is that tactic helping you right now? Maybe you don't need the bigger picture."

My mouth fell open. I felt it drop as the weight of what she'd said hit me.

"Uh, huh," Florry said. "Starting to get it now, are you? This isn't normal human life, girly. You have to think differently."

"I'm going to try that," I said.

"Good," she grunted, and I saw her form begin to fade away.

"Wait!" I held out a hand, like I could grab onto her and stop her from leaving.

"What?" She wasn't pleased.

"How did you die?" I asked, thinking about what blond and nasty had said.

"What?"

"How did you die?" I repeated. "I read your note in the back of the grimoire," I said.

"You did?" Florry was pleased. "I wasn't sure when it would be shown to you."

"It was one of the first pages I was able to read. Did you know you were dying?"

"The Oracles can live for a long time. We don't age like everyone else. There have been a number of us who have chosen to die, because we're tired. I wasn't quite there, but I was slowing down. I liked sleeping in later, where before I was up with the sun. And I had a feeling. You'll get used to that, too, girly," she said, pointing the Olympia can at me. "Listen to your feelings. So I wrote the note, because I wanted to be sure I added my bit, just in case."

"So how did you die?"

"I don't know," Florry said.

Unlike the vague answers she'd given before, this one didn't make me question whether or not she was withholding information. "You don't know?" I breathed.

She shook her head. "Nope. Don't have a clue. I went to bed one night, and then when I woke up, I could tell I was in between. It's got a different feeling. You felt it, didn't you? When you came to see me?"

I nodded.

"There you go. I don't know how I died. Maybe Goldie knew it was time, and he left."

"Let's ask him," I said, holding out my arm.

I don't know, I heard Goldie say. *I remember Florry going to sleep, and the next thing I knew, I was in a bag. Then I was pulled out by Ashton Flint, right before you found me.*

"You don't remember anything else?"

No, I do not, Goldie said.

"What'd he say?" Florry asked.

I told her, and got up, unable to sit still. "This doesn't strike either of you as really sketchy?" I asked. "Neither of you remember?"

"Sometimes the Oracle just passes away," Florry said. "It happens."

"There's more to it than that," I insisted. I didn't know how I knew, but I knew there was more than just a simple death.

"Sometimes there is, and sometimes there isn't," Florry said. "If you feel strongly about it, you need to keep that in your head as you're working through your Logan problem."

"My Logan problem," I groaned. "I still don't know how to give him the answers he's looking for."

"Get in the party, and stop looking at the big picture," Florry said. "I'm out of here." She disappeared.

"Looks like it's you and me," I said to Goldie.

I do not like that man that came close to you earlier today. He's not a good man, Goldie said.

"I agree," I said.

I know you have your doubts about your new role, Goldie continued. *Whatever they are, please do not give me to him.*

"I do have doubts," I said. "You're right. I have a lot of them. I won't give you to him, though. He gives me the creeps."

Trust your instinct, Goldie said.

"And what else?" I asked.

He didn't respond.

"Why do you guys always leave right in the middle of a good conversation?" I asked out loud.

There was no answer.

I thought over Florry's comment. What was the deal with all these people hinted at by blond villain guy, and whatever that bull had been? Why were they after the Oracle once it came to me? What was it about me?

My insecurity could give that all sorts of answers, but I didn't think that would be helpful.

"All right. Get in the party, she said. See the smaller rather than the bigger picture." I went to the kitchen and got out the herbs and the burner. "Worth a try."

CHAPTER TWELVE

I lay on the couch, my eyes closed, the fragrant herbs filling the air around me. I pictured the party, in the room with dark walls, and chandeliers, and magic moving through the room, all kinds of magic. It was amazing and scary and fascinating all at once.

Join the party, I thought. I pictured my sea foam dress, but longer, like a ball gown, in satin and chiffon. When I looked down, I could see the fabric of the dress floating around my ankles. Silver heels with straps covered in rhinestones finished off the outfit. I had a small silver clutch in my hand.

I wished I could see myself. Just because the dress was so beautiful.

At that moment, a tall man, his hair a light honey blond, bumped into me. He looked down, and the admiration in his eyes was clear. "Pardon me, madam. I am Tomas Severn, at your service." He inclined his head crisply. "Might I know your name, and maybe invite you to dance?"

"I'm Wynter," I said. "Wynter Chastain."

"Miss Wynter," his eyes warmed. "It is indeed a pleasure. Please, accompany me for a dance." He held out his hand.

I took it, and let him lead me to where couples were twirling in the middle of the room. This was good. It would allow me to move through the room without attracting excess attention. I looked like just another party guest.

"I haven't seen you at one of these events before," Tomas said. "What brings you here?"

Oh. Crap. "It was a last minute invitation," I said, putting on my brightest smile. "I was lucky not to have any other engagements this evening. What about you? Do you attend regularly?" I hoped I wasn't asking the wrong kind of questions.

"When I can," Tomas said, and a shifty expression moved across his face. It made him look less handsome.

"This is a good place to meet like-minded people," he added.

"Absolutely," I said, and let my eyes fall downward, almost as though I were shy.

He chuckled. "Ah, Miss Wynter, I believe we could be very like-minded, indeed."

Okay, eww. He moved from handsome man to definitely creepy. I didn't say anything, nor did I look up at him. I needed to find an exit.

"The entertainment is beginning," Tomas said. "Look up. They put on a spectacular show here."

When I raised my eyes, I could see colorful clouds of sparkling light above us. It was forming and reforming, and every time it reformed, it had a more defined shape. Eventually, there were three peacocks, all blue and green and gold, dancing above us, tails waving in an invisible wind.

The crowd murmured appreciatively. The dancing had stopped as people watched the show above.

I glanced around. The small group I'd been watching was off to my left, and the four men who had projected menace every time I saw them were all gazing toward the ceiling as well.

But the man with his back to me was bent down, whispering into the ear of a dark haired woman in blue. The woman in gold, with blond hair, was at his other side, her arm threaded through his, a look of displeasure on her face.

"Excuse me," I said to Tomas. "The crush," I added as I moved away from him, trying to get over to the seven people I'd been watching for what seemed like ages.

Moving in that direction was easier said than done. Every time I made progress, I was forced to sidestep or even move backward. When I finally took more than five steps, I found that I was all turned around, and I'd lost sight of the man with his back to me.

I knew then, as sure as I knew my name, that I had to get to him, and quickly. He was in danger. If I didn't help him, warn him, something—I would never be able to help Logan. I didn't know how I knew, but I knew.

Trust your instinct, Goldie had said.

My gut was screaming at me.

I took another five or six steps, and saw the woman in the gold dress. My heart leapt with excitement. I was close. I stepped around a man and a woman who were arm in arm, reaching out. Maybe I could get to him before the four men with ill intent turned their attention to him once more.

I blinked as the light in the room flashed, almost like a strobe light. Then I looked up and I was staring into Logan's eyes.

I screamed.

He jumped back, his hands out in front of him. "Holy hell, Wynter!"

I sat up. "What happened?" I asked. I was lying on the couch, and wearing the same clothes I'd been wearing when I went shopping. When I laid down to try and direct my vision.

Logan shrugged, keeping his distance and eyeing me warily. "I rang and rang the doorbell, but you didn't answer. The door wasn't locked either," he added with a glare. "You need to stop leaving it open. So I came in, and you were lying there, muttering and thrashing around. Then you yelled something, although I couldn't tell what you were saying, and that's when I woke you up."

I fell back, feeling the tears spring to my eyes. "I was so close," I said.

"To what?"

I let the tears fall, feeling the weight of all that had happened today. "It has not been a good day," I said. "Not in any way."

"What happened?" His entire demeanor shifted, and I could see the panther within him stir. His eyes took on a golden sheen around the outside of the iris' normal green coloring.

I told him about the blond guy, and what he'd said. His face darkened as I continued to speak. Then I told him about Hazel Babbington and her minions, and he laughed.

"I would have liked to have seen her gasping like a fish. You responded to that well. To both of the people who accosted you," Logan added. "You should be proud of yourself."

"Is there something about me that makes you think I'd be steamrolled?"

"What?" Logan looked taken aback by the sudden shift in subject.

"My guide asked me why I thought these people who want to take the Oracle from me were drawn to me. She didn't experience any of this when she became the Oracle."

His brows furrowed. "I haven't thought about it like that, to be honest."

"Well, me neither, but I've been thinking about it ever since she asked me. Do I seem weak?"

"No," his response was immediate. "You aren't sure of what's going on, or what you're supposed to do. That's not weakness, though. I don't get weakness from you at all, and I can usually smell it on people."

"You have super smelling as well as super hearing powers?" I asked. God, was I stinky?

"Yes," he said. "And weakness has an aroma. You're not weak, Wynter," Logan said. "Maybe it's because you're on the verge of a lot of power?" His eyebrows went up.

"You think?"

He shrugged. "I get a lot of power from you, even though you're not really using it. It's there, though. Like, it's waiting."

"Thank you," I said, swinging my legs onto the floor. "I think I need some water, and a really big cup of tea."

"I can help you with that," Logan said.

"No, I got it," I waved him off. I walked toward the kitchen, glancing out the front window, and stopped dead in my tracks. "What in the heck," I began as I walked to the window.

Carefully, I peeked out, not wanting to move the lace curtains, or let on that I was looking out.

"What?" Logan was behind me.

"That van," I said.

"What about it?"

"Navy blue, no windows, chrome bumpers. I'd bet there is a slight dent in the rear driver's side bumper," I said, squinting at the van that was parked across the street.

"What is the deal with the van?"

"When I found the grimoire, that looks exactly like the van that was in the parking lot near the cemetery in Danvers," I said. "And..." I stopped, remembering. "When Ash and I were walking out of the The Black Dog, a van like this went racing past us. Now it's here, in front of my house? Without anyone in the seats?" I turned around, my indignation growing.

"It could just be a van, Wynter," Logan said.

"I don't think so," I said. I walked to the door, reaching for my shoes.

"Hey, what are you doing?"

"If this is that blond jerk who tried to scare me in the grocery store, I'm going to give him a piece of my mind. While I'm calling the cops," I said.

"No, don't do that, Wynter."

"Why not?" I rounded on Logan. "I'm tired of people stalking me, trying to direct me to do what they want. To push me around. This is my life, and I'm the only one who gets to make decisions. Good or bad, that's my choice!"

"I get it, I hear you," Logan said. "Let me go out and get rid of them."

"My kids are coming tomorrow. I don't want that van here when they come. I don't want them seeing my kids, knowing who they are. They already know too much."

"Wynter, you don't know that this is a threat."

"Yes, I do," I said. "I know."

He gazed at me for a moment, then nodded. "All right. I'll trust your gut. Let's leave them here tonight, and I'll go scare the hell out of them after dark. Will that work?"

Having seen his panther at rest, I couldn't even imagine his panther pissed off. "I think that would be great."

"Okay. Why don't you—"

I waved a hand. "I'm going to make dinner, and then I'll go upstairs and read for a while."

Logan knew not to push. "All right. Just give a shout if you need anything." And then he was gone.

I pulled out the ingredients for white chicken chili. It was fast, and I could toss it in my pressure cooker, and be done with it. I cut and chopped and stirred with a vengeance, the anger at being harassed refusing to leave. Then I started the pressure cooker, set the time, and went upstairs.

I immediately pulled out the grimoire. "I need to know how to get rid of people who are trying to scare me, trying to make me do what they want," I said.

I thumbed through the grimoire twice, but no new pages appeared. Damn it. This was so frustrating.

I could hear the beeping of the pressure cooker, and I went back downstairs to find Logan peering at it.

"What do I need to do?" he asked.

"You've never used a pressure cooker?" The thought made me smile for the first time since I'd seen the van.

"A crock pot, yes. This, no."

"Well, the old time pressure cookers could blow up in your face," I said.

Logan stepped back, a look of alarm on his face.

"But the new ones are a lot safer. Here, let's let off the steam, and then it will be ready."

"What is it? It smells awesome."

"White chicken chili," I said. While the cooker was venting, I got the sliced avocados, the sour cream, the shredded cheese, and the tortilla strips out, setting them on the island.

"So this is really an entire meal disguised as soup."

"Yes," I said. "It's one of my favorites." When the cooker finished, I dished out large bowls for us both.

We sat down at the island, not speaking as we added all the yum to the chili. Logan took a bite, then another. "This is delicious," he said.

"Glad you like it." Some of my earlier rage was fading.

"What do you want me to do if I find someone magic or supernatural in the van?"

"What can you do?" I asked.

"I can scare the hell out of them, or worse," he said, watching me carefully.

"I don't want them to die. Not unless they try and hurt me, or the kids."

"Do you still have the card the guy gave you?"

I nodded. "Why?"

"Let me smell it. I'll be able to tell if he's in the van."

I immediately got up and went to fish it out of my purse.

"Easy," Logan said, laughing. "You have time to eat. It's not even dark yet." But he took it as I slid it over to him.

By tacit agreement, we didn't talk about the van, or my dreams, or his quest, or anything else. We talked about food, and my kids, and how they were doing with the loss of Derek. It was nice. It was normal.

After dinner, I cleaned up. It had gotten dark while we ate, and I was antsy.

Logan did a lap around the house. "There's no one near your place." He picked up the card from the island, and inhaled deeply with it right next to his nose.

Then his nose wrinkled and he coughed. "God, this guy stinks."

"What does that mean?"

"He does magic, and whatever it is, it stinks. I can't tell any more than that. But if he's in the van, I won't be able to miss him."

"Are you going to shift?"

"I think I'll try the face to face approach first, and hint that you have more allies."

"I like that," I said.

"It's better if they think it's more than you and me," Logan said. "All right. Sit tight. I'll be back soon."

I found that I couldn't sit still. I turned off the lights and moved into the front room, where I peered out the curtains.

I saw Logan approach the van. He stood at the window, speaking to someone within.

And then the magic all around the van, around Logan, swelled. I could see it. It was dark blue, and black, and angry and scary.

Someone reached out of the van to push Logan in the chest, and the van took off.

Logan stood in the middle of the street, watching. Then he turned and jogged back toward the house. He didn't come up to the front door, but ran around the back, and came in via the porch and kitchen door.

"Who was it?" I demanded.

"The man who threatened you had been there at some point. I couldn't tell if he was in there, but his stink was all over the place. It was just one guy, older and tired, hanging out. I asked what he was doing and he told me, very rudely, to mind my own business." He grinned.

"I saw him push you."

"Ah, he's an old guy. That's not the one we want. But he will go back and tell Stinky, and that should buy you some time so your kids can come and go before they come back."

"That's what I want, thank you," I said. The rage at this guy's nerve hit me again, but if I could keep him from seeing my kids, I could manage it.

This was when I wanted some kind of skill, any skill, that could protect me and mine.

I went to bed mad, and when I dreamed, I was no good in the party dream. I couldn't get into the dream like I had earlier. Then I felt my feet start to warm, and I knew a hot flash was on the way.

That was a sign. It was time to stop, and try and sleep. I wet a washcloth in cold water, got back into bed, and fell asleep with it on my face.

CHAPTER THIRTEEN

"Tell Shelly thank you," I said to Logan.

"I will. You've reminded me at least half a dozen times," Logan said patiently.

"Okay. I'll call later. Probably not until tomorrow. They will probably want to spend the night."

"I'll come by after dark, make sure that no one is lurking," he said. Then with a smile, he was gone.

The house seemed too quiet after Logan left. I'd really enjoyed having the kids out of the house, but now, after having Logan there for a few days, it was too quiet.

That offered some suggestions that I wasn't ready to consider. Were you supposed to get this close and friendly with your consultants? I thought about calling out for Florry, but two cars pulled into the driveway.

The kids were here.

They all came in together, not talking. That wasn't a good sign. I got up and hugged them, one at a time.

Still nothing.

"All right. Let's sit down, and talk about it," I said. Then I went to the couch, sat, and waited.

Surprisingly, it wasn't Rachel who took the lead. It was Kris. "We've been talking, Mom."

"Okay," I said.

"You paid for college. You helped us get set up. I know, none of us bought a house. I hate to tell you, that's not going to happen for a while. Mom, we're fine. All three of us," he said.

I looked to Rachel and Theo. They nodded.

"This isn't what I wanted," I said.

"We know that. But you and Dad did a lot for us. Now things are different, and you have to live the rest of your life without Dad, without an income."

"I don't want you to have to go out and get a job now," Rachel said. "Not after being home all these years.

Some loser company will totally take advantage of you."

"Is that what you think?"

"Maybe," Theo said. "It's vicious out there right now."

"Well, I appreciate your concern, even if I have to wonder if you think I'm a bit of a simpleton," I said. "However, as I've taken up a hobby, volunteering to help people who have lost things—"

"What kind of hobby is that?" Kris interrupted.

"Mine," I said firmly. "We work with a lot of older folk. Through a senior center."

I didn't imagine the looks of relief all three kids shared with one another. They were trying to be discreet, and failing miserably. If I wasn't kind of offended, I would be touched.

It was better they thought I was doing something with a senior center. Poor old Mom. Not fit for the working world. Was that what all my years got me? I'd run Derek's entire business—I stopped myself.

It was all right that they thought this. We'd made sure that they didn't ever see the business side. And honestly, given that I'd missed an entire family, I didn't want them to see me as part of the business side.

"As it happens, if I wanted a job, I could get one doing bookkeeping yesterday," I said. "I kept all your dad's books, and I did all the accounting. So I haven't been out of the working world." I wondered if Derek had another set of books. Or if I'd been the one cooking his books, lying about the money, so that he had enough for both families? I only had the information he gave me—and I thought about going back, looking into contracts, then stopped.

It didn't matter anymore. He'd hidden Natalie and the kids from us, and that was that. What mattered was what we did now.

"When did you have time to work?" Rachel asked. "You were always busy taking care of the house, and us."

"I'm an excellent multitasker," I said.

Which made all three of them laugh.

"Fine, fine. We'll leave you alone and stop being condescending jerks," Theo said, still laughing. "It came from a good place, Mom. We love you."

"I love you, too." I got up, and walked toward the window. There was no one out there, not even a neighbor walking their dog. No van, no scary blond guy. But I felt my skin crawling.

Something was off.

I rubbed my hands along my arms.

"What's wrong?" Kris came up behind me.

"Oh, I'm just being silly. It's hard to believe Dad is gone."

"Well, it's a good thing, in some ways. I might have to kill him," Rachel said grimly. "How could he do this? To you? To us?"

"To those other kids?" Theo asked.

I noted that none of them mentioned Natalie. Well, they could be mad at her. That wasn't on me to fix. They were entitled to their anger.

"I don't know," I said. "I haven't gone through his closet, or any of his things. I don't know if he left a note, or anything else."

"We can do that now, if you want," Rachel said, her voice much softer.

I thought about it. I'd been wanting to get his stuff out of the closet, out of our dresser. The piles of clothes I'd tossed on the floor. "All right," I said. "I appreciate it, if you three are up to it."

When we got into the closet, Rachel stopped. "Mom, what's going on?" She was looking down at the pile of clothing I'd yanked from their hangers after Cody visited.

"What do you mean?" I tried to keep it light.

"You look different than when I saw you last week." She peered at me. "It's like, you're sparkling." She didn't mention the clothing.

"Oh," I said. Oh, no, I thought. Was that magic, or the Oracle, or something to do with Goldie making itself known?

"Don't you think so?" Rachel turned to Theo. "Doesn't Mom have a sparkly thing going on?"

"She always has," Kris came in. "It's just that it's back now."

It was all I could do not to cry, right there, in the middle of Derek's closet.

"Mom, what happened here?" Theo looked around at the mess I'd left.

"Oh, I was upset," I waved it away. "I just never got around to picking it up."

"Good thing we're here," Kris said, chuckling.

And that was that. No other comments about me tossing Derek's clothes around. Which I appreciated. We spent the rest of the afternoon going through the master bedroom. Kris went out and got some boxes, and together, we folded up Derek's clothes, placing them into the boxes. "You can take whatever you want," I said. "I don't mind."

After that, all three made a pile, which I was glad to see. This would always be their dad, despite his glaring flaws.

As the day went on, we got through all the things in the closet. Theo was dusting one of the cabinets when he let out a yelp.

"What?" I asked, heading into the closet.

"There's a door in the bottom of the cabinet," he said, his head still inside the cabinet. He popped out. "Do you have one in your closet, Mom?"

I shook my head.

Kris and Rachel came to stand on either side of me. "Well, let's open it," I said.

He pulled open the small door, and peered in. Then he brought out a thin black metal box. Theo looked at me.

"Open that, too," I said.

Inside was a large cream envelope that filled the entire box.

In Case of My Death was scrawled across the front in Derek's spiky handwriting.

Theo handed me the envelope, and I opened it. I wasn't sure if I wanted to know what was in here, what he had to say for himself. But I opened it anyway.

There were four smaller envelopes in it, each with one of our names. I passed them out, and then looked at mine.

"Don't you want to open it?" Rachel asked.

"No. I don't. I think I'll open it later, when I'm on my own. Let's get this finished," I said briskly. "We're almost done."

It only took us another hour. Theo and Kris brought the boxes down to Theo's car, promising to drop them at our local charity shop. Then we all sat down to dinner. I'd made a huge pot of the white chicken chili the night before, and it was just as good the second time around.

Everyone went to bed early, eager, no doubt to read their letters in peace. We hadn't talked about Natalie, or what to do next with regard to her and the kids, but that would come.

Maybe it would be more clear after we all read Derek's last words.

I took a long time getting ready for bed. I called Shelly, and told her that Logan would need to stay the night, that it had been a long day, and I'd fill her in later. She didn't ask questions. "Take care of yourself, too, honey. It's not just the kids that need some TLC."

"Thanks, Shell," I said.

"Love ya, girl."

"Love you, too," I said.

We hung up.

The letter from Derek sat on the other side of the bed, on his side of the bed. I glared at it for a time, then finally picked it up.

Dear Wynter,

If you're reading this, you found my box, and I'm gone. You know about the insurance policy, and you've learned about Natalie, Sophie, and Nathan. There's nothing else to say to you but that I'm sorry.

I wanted to tell you. I wanted to be honest so many times, but why should you have been hurt because I was too much of a coward to make a decision? The problem was, I loved you both. Then when Sophie and Nathan came along, I couldn't walk away.

Natalie didn't know. She had no idea. All the time I spent with you, she thought I worked with a museum in Boston. It was just part of my life, and she accepted that from the beginning.

I'm sorry. I am so, so sorry. I hope that someday, all of my kids will be able to sit down together. I've loved them with everything I had, from the moment they were born to the last time I gave them a hug and a kiss. I tried to explain to each of the kids, but who knows how that will go?

Don't be mad about the money, Wynter. You got the business. If you did things the way we planned, you got a good price for it. Natalie needs to get the kids raised, get them through school. I know they're not your concern, but I love them as much as I love Theo, Rachel, and Kris.

And I love you. I've loved you since the first time I met you in college. I've loved everything about you. I would have never thought I had the capacity to love two amazing women, and be enough for both of them, but I did. I never stopped loving you.

Take care of yourself, and know that I was with you to the end.

Love,

Derek

I tossed the letter across the bed, tears streaming down my face. The nerve of him! To try and make his lies, his years and years of lies, sound noble.

But in his words, I also read truth. He had loved me. He loved Natalie. And while the thought of sharing a man with another woman made me recoil, Derek had told me his truth. I didn't have to like it. I didn't. I would have kicked him in the butt until my leg fell off if I'd discovered this while he was alive.

It was, however, his truth.

God, I wondered how my kids were doing. I wanted to go to them, to each of them, to hold them like I'd held them when they fell down when they were younger, but that wouldn't be the fix all that it had been.

If they wanted to see me, they'd come to see me.

I cried myself to sleep for knowing the truth, and knowing I could never pretend again.

The next morning, I was up before any of my children, making coffee, tea, and a big breakfast. They all came down within ten minutes of each other. I didn't ask any of them what their dad had written to them. That was for them, and them alone.

"He's the worst," Rachel said. Her eyes were red and swollen.

"Yeah, this didn't make it better," Kris said.

"I don't know," Theo began.

Kris and Rachel both turned to him, their glances accusing.

"Mom?" Theo asked.

"If he'd been in front of me when I read his letter, I might have snatched him bald," I said. "No one wants to hear your husband has another family that he loves. But if he had to be like this, I think he did the best he could. And that's all the grace I can give him," I said.

"What do you want to do about Natalie?" Rachel demanded.

"And the kids?" Theo asked.

"He said Natalie didn't know," I began.

"Do you believe him?" Rachel crossed her arms, scowling. It was obvious she didn't.

"I don't know. I don't have any reason not to. I mean, he wrote that letter, all these letters, thinking he would be dead and gone. He didn't have to face a thing," I said. "So there was no reason for him to lie."

"You're nicer than me," Rachel said.

"Maybe," I said. "I do not need to get in touch with Natalie. I don't need to meet her, I don't have a burning desire to yell at her, or shake my fist in her face, or any of that. If you three want to meet your siblings, however, I am all for it, and I'll send her a message."

The three of them exchanged glances. With them being so close in age, they had fought like cats and dogs when they were younger. Now, they were strong and united. I loved to see it.

"I'd like to meet them," Kris said.

"So would I," said Theo.

Rachel, arms still crossed, only nodded.

I let out a breath I didn't know I'd been holding. "All right. Then let's write Mrs. Chastain a letter."

"Not funny," Kris said.

"I have to start seeing it as kind of funny," I said. "Or I'm going to curl up and die in a ball of bitterness."

"Well, when you put it that way," Rachel said.

"Just keeping it real," I said.

We spent the next two hours composing a letter that everyone was happy with. While the kids went up and packed, I typed it up. I went to Natalie's social media, and found an email. Then I got the email ready, stopping to read it once more.

Dear Natalie,

You don't know us, but by now, you've probably heard our names. I'm Wynter Chastain, Derek's wife. We were married for twenty-five years, and until the life insurance policy signatures were needed, I had no idea that he had built a life with you and your children as well. I know this has been hard on me, and our three children. I imagine it's been similar for you. The truth between our families is awful and painful, and I am so sorry to have to contact you in this way, with all that is between us.

I do have a reason for this email. My children, Theo, Rachel, and Kris, very much wish to meet their siblings. They know that your children have also lost their father. I have told them I'll support their wishes, as long as you are willing to be a part of this. If you decide that you'd rather not, all of us will respect that decision. I'll tell you, with all honesty, I hope to hear from you soon.

Sincerely,

Wynter Chastain

It didn't feel perfect, but I'd decided that there was nothing that would feel completely right in this situation. How could it? There was so much hurt to be navigated. I didn't feel comfortable, but since there was no Emily Post to give me a guide, this was what the kids and I had come up with. Simple and the truth.

Theo was down first. "Did you send it?"

"Not yet," I said. "I wanted all of you to read it once more."

He nodded.

One by one, my children read the email that marked the end of the life that we'd known, the life we thought we had. For that, for taking that away from them, I wasn't sure that I'd ever be able to forgive Derek. They deserved better. I deserved better.

But I was so proud of my children. Even through this, they were being good people, good humans, never forgetting there was another family, like ours, that was neck deep in hurt, and just trying to find their way through the situation we all had to live with.

Derek may have betrayed me, but we'd done a great job with our kids.

"It's good," Rachel said, tears shimmering in her eyes.

Kris nodded.

"Well, all right then." I hit Send, and the email disappeared. A moment later, a ding came from the laptop, letting me know that the email had been successfully sent.

"All we can do now is wait," I said.

They all hugged me more than once, and then Kris and Theo left together. Rachel had driven herself, and she waved at me as she backed out of the driveway.

Then they were gone.

I closed the door and went back inside. "Goodbye, Derek," I said. And I closed the door on my marriage.

I slept deeply that night, not dreaming of anything.

When I woke the next morning, it was as though a veil had been removed from my eyes. I got out of bed, and called Shelly. "You can get rid of him now," I said to her.

She laughed. "No, he can stay for as long as he wants," she said.

"You are awful," I said, laughing at her tone.

"Seriously, he's a nice man. I enjoyed his company. How did it go with the kids?"

"They are rock stars, Shell. Such good people. Way better than me and Derek."

"That's how it's supposed to be, honey. What did you all decide?"

"I sent her an email."

"Then you've done all you can. Now what's next on the schedule?"

"Send Logan over. You can come too, if you like. I'm going to find out who he is today. Did Logan tell you about all the threats?"

"Yes, he did. Although you should have been the one to do that telling, missy. And he told me about that hateful Hazel Babbington."

"Oh, god," I groaned. "You know she's telling everyone the worst possible things."

"I happen to be on the Beautification Council with her," Shelly said. "We have a meeting today. Normally, I skip them unless we have an official vote, because it's a bunch of nasty gossips like Hazel, but I think I'll go today, and see what folks are saying."

"Thank you," I said. Even with all my new focus, I still had to live here. And when I gave up the Oracle, I wouldn't have anything else. I knew Shelly was going to go in guns blazing on my behalf.

"It is absolutely my pleasure. Now I'll send your guy over. Good luck with whatever you all are working on today," Shelly said.

She ended the call.

I set up the burner, and got my herbs ready. I meant what I said. I was going to find out who the man who kept his back to me was, and why I had to know that before I could help Logan. I'd have to go and get more herbs if I didn't quite manage it today.

The doorbell rang, and I yelled out, "Come in."

CHAPTER FOURTEEN

I heard both doors open. "I'm almost ready," I said, not looking up. "I think today is the day we find out—" I turned and then stopped.

My blood turned to ice.

In front of me, with a horrible smile on his face, was the blond man, the one Logan called Stinky.

"Mrs. Chastain. It appears you've chosen to ignore my very sage and heartfelt advice," he said softly, the menace clear in every word.

"I have," I said, standing up straight and trying not to let him see how scared I was.

Get out, Goldie said. *You need to get out now. You are no match for him.*

"Wynter," I heard Florry somewhere in the background.

But I couldn't take my eyes off the man.

"They can't help you," he said, his tone almost apologetic. Almost. There was too much glee for him to really be apologetic. He was enjoying this. "I warned you."

Oh, god. I wished he would leave. I closed my eyes, trying to remember if I'd seen anything about stopping someone who planned to kill you from doing it. But I didn't know what he was going to do, or how he planned it. I didn't know what kind of magic he was using, and even if I did, I had no way to defend against it.

I had nothing.

I'm sorry, I thought. *Goldie, I'm sorry. I tried. Tell Florry to tell my kids I love them.*

Goldie said something, but I couldn't hear it. The blond man began to chant, and the anger and danger in his words filled the room, swirling around like an evil tornado. The magic came all around me, and I couldn't move. I couldn't do anything.

"No," I said out loud. I couldn't even hear myself speak.

The blond man came closer. Black tendrils stretched from his hands, working their inky way toward me. They were like smoke, only they had a quality that made me think of something far worse.

The blond man kept chanting as I watched. He and his tendrils came closer.

Damn it. I was finally getting the hang of this Oracle thing, or at least, I wasn't falling on my face passing out anymore. And now this guy was coming in here? He was going to kill me, taking my talking snake armband, and my ghost, and the peace I'd found with my kids.

Over my dead body.

Which was no doubt his plan.

But that didn't mean I had to go along with it.

I stretched out my hands. "No. Stay back," I shouted.

He kept chanting.

"Get back," I screamed. "Get back, get back!"

His eyes had a reddish tint, and I could swear that I saw fangs as he grinned evilly at me.

"Nooo!" I screamed, wanting to push him away from me, get him out of my house, out of my neighborhood, out of my town, gone forever.

The magic swirled around me even more ferociously, a whine rising in my ears that hurt. I screamed in protest, and closed my eyes, imagining stinky blond guy far away from here.

In the middle of a desert. Anywhere but here, preferably somewhere he couldn't easily escape from.

The noise around me stopped.

Oh, god. Was I dead? I was afraid to open my eyes. But I had to.

I was still in my living room. The place was a mess. Blond guy was nowhere to be seen.

The front door banged open, and then Logan came in, his eyes wild and gold. He was on the verge of shifting. "Are you all right?"

"I... I think so," I said shakily.

"Where is he? I smelled him before I even hit the walkway."

I shook my head. "I don't know."

Logan looked at me in disbelief.

"Seriously, I don't know," I said.

"Wynter," I heard Florry behind me. "What did you do?"

"I don't know," I said. "I was wishing he was anywhere else but here."

Florry came close to me, looking me up and down. "I think your magic just made an appearance."

"You think?" I asked.

"What is going on?" Logan demanded.

"Florry thinks I just used magic and got rid of my stinky problem." I couldn't believe the words even as I said them.

Logan didn't reply, but ran from the room. I heard him move through the house, and then upstairs. He came back down, and ran outside.

When he returned, he said, "He's not here."

"You did this," Florry said. "You're going to need to do some homework tonight."

"You don't know what this is?"

"What, do I look like a GPS? Some sort of mapping system?" Florry demanded. "I told you, every Oracle must find her own way. This is yours. So it's up to you to see where it goes."

"Helpful to the end," I muttered. Now that he was gone, that I wasn't looking at my own death, I felt myself start to shake. "I think I need to sit down."

"Have a drink," Florry advised. "I'm going to." As if to make her point, I heard her open a can of beer.

"What do you need?" Logan asked.

"I think I need a healthy amount of scotch, and then I need to go to bed."

He brought me over what had to be at least a double. I sat on the edge of the couch and drank every last drop. "Logan, I wanted to work on deciphering more of the vision, but I think I need to wait until tomorrow," I said once I'd finished the scotch.

"That's fine," Logan said. His face was worried, but he was trying to keep it to himself.

"All right," I said. Carefully, I walked past him, ignoring the mess that was my house, and made my way up the stairs. I crawled into bed, and pulled the blankets up to my chin. "I don't want to dream," I said. "Not today."

Then I closed my eyes.

*W*hile I slept, Logan cleaned my house. He'd called Shelly, who promptly made way too much food. By the time I woke up, I had a fridge full of dinner, and two very worried people on the couch, watching me anxiously as I came down the stairs.

They have been very concerned, Goldie said.

I know, I thought. *And you?*

I knew you would be well. But whatever it is you have done, you expended a great deal of energy. You will need to remember that should you wish to use that much magic again.

I just need to know what it was I did, I thought. I hadn't looked in the grimoire since I'd gone up to bed. That was on the agenda today.

"Honey, how are you?" Shelly got up, rushing to hug me. "I've talked to all your kids. They know you aren't feeling well, but they think it's just a little bit of flu. They're all good."

"No sign of Stinky," Logan came to stand next to her. "No blue van, either. In fact, it's been positively boring."

"You shameful man," Shelly slapped at his arm. "I've been here the entire time."

I laughed. "Thank you, both of you."

After I'd sat down, and eaten far too much, I turned to Logan. "Has your person been able to break into the account?" I asked.

He nodded. "Almost. I just wanted to make sure that you were up and around. I'm going to go and see him, see if we can track it down. He said there are a lot of layers."

"What does that mean?" Shelly asked.

"It means someone went to a lot of trouble to hide the owner of the account," Logan said grimly.

"I think you—we're—close," I said.

"Is that like an official Oracle pronouncement?" Logan asked.

I considered his question. "Yes, I think it is."

"Good. That makes me feel a little better. This shouldn't take long. I'll let you know when I get there, and then what I find out."

"And I'll stay with you," Shelly said.

"I'm going to be fine," I protested.

"Shut up and let me do this," she replied. "I thought you were going to die."

"Well, when you play dirty like that," I said.

"Darn right," Shelly said.

Logan left within the hour, eager to be on his way. I meant what I'd said. I felt like we were close.

"What do you want to do today?" Shelly asked.

"You know, I don't want to do anything related to Oracle stuff. You want to help in my garden?"

"Sounds perfect," Shelly said.

We walked into the back yard together, needing no conversation.

I was more at peace than I'd been since Derek died.

We were going to be all right. All of us.

I could feel it.

CHAPTER FIFTEEN

I spent the next two days worrying for Logan. I knew that he had to go, that he had to check out his hacker source. I knew it like I knew my kids. That's how sure I was. But not knowing if he was all right, or if something had happened—I was a mess. I hadn't heard anything since he'd left. He didn't check in. And when one day stretched into two —my sense of foreboding grew. The garden had provided some respite the first day he left. After that, however, I couldn't sit still. I tried to watch a movie, to read a book, to look for what sort of magic it was that I'd used in the grimoire, but I wasn't able to settle my mind. I was pretty sure that was why the grimoire didn't show me diddly squat. It wanted my full attention.

I didn't have it to give.

I burned the herbs like crazy, trying to see something more, something different than I'd seen at the party before. I got the feeling I was running out of time.

Finally, he sent me a text. He would be back later tonight. He had news. I could feel it. Knowing that he was safe, and had maybe made some progress, I was able to relax, and I think that was what made the difference. I lit the tea light, and inhaled the burning herbs. I fell right into the party dream. I forced myself to move around, to try and find details, and every night, I tried to get close to the man whose face I couldn't see. So far, I hadn't succeeded. Tonight, I walked around in the gardens, and even out in the front, wanting to get an idea of the house. It was a jackpot move, because I saw the house number. 529. Then I grabbed one of the valets that was hurrying by. "What is the street name here?" I asked.

You'd think I'd know, since I was at the house, but he didn't seem to see anything wrong with my question. "We're at 529 Van der Veere Way. Right outside of Old Forge."

"Thank you," I said.

He nodded, and moved past me.

Now that I knew where we were, it was time to figure out the who part of this mystery. I was going to see the man who kept his back to me tonight if it killed me.

Well, maybe not if it killed me. I'd already risked that once recently. I wasn't keen to do it again. But I was going to get to him. I saw Tomas, and took the long way around the ballroom to avoid him, making a beeline for the seven people I'd been trying to get closer to.

As the magical light peacocks began to dance in the air above, I slid around people, trying not to get caught up. I could see my quarry, with the two women on either side of him. Then something different happened. The woman in blue moved away, stopping to stand between two of the four men who'd been around the man with his back to me.

The woman in gold wasted no time, reaching for him, running her hand along his broad shoulder.

I was six feet away, then four, then three, and—I ran into him.

He turned and as he did, I saw the blonde woman, a pale cool face with very red lipstick, sneering at me. "Watch where you're going," she all but hissed.

"I'm sorry," I said, putting up one hand to steady myself on the man I'd been dreaming of. The man who was the answer, the key to helping my consultant.

Logan Gentry stared down at me, a bemused, somewhat distant smile on his face. "It's no bother," he began, and then he must have seen the expression my face.

I couldn't speak. I was pretty sure my mouth was open, because the blonde rolled her eyes and flipped her hair.

"Really," she said.

"Have we met?" Logan-not-Logan asked. His hair was short, cut close to his head, and darker, but lightened in the way people's hair lightened in the sun. I could tell that he spent a lot of money on this haircut. Everything about him screamed money. A lot of money. Bushels of it. Whatever he'd been doing, he was very, very successful.

"Oh, Evander, please," the blonde said.

He held up a hand in her direction and she closed her mouth. That meant he was powerful, as well, even with all the hate and ill will that came his way from his male companions.

"I'm Evander Thane," he said.

"Wynter Chastain," I stuck out my hand.

Logan-Evander took my hand and with agonizing slowness, brought it to his lips. The thrill that his touch sent through every molecule of my body was enough to drop me where I stood.

"It is my pleasure, Wynter," Logan-Evander said. Unlike when Tomas had said something similar, I didn't get creep vibes.

Although whatever Logan-Evander was involved with, it was some shady business. I knew that without any doubt whatsoever.

"What brings you to this party this evening?" Logan-Evander asked. "As we haven't met, and we're cele-brating my latest find this evening."

"And your next commission," the blonde woman said, tightening her arm around Logan-Evander's.

"Davina, please," he said, without even turning to look at her. At the same time, he gracefully extracted his arm from her clutches.

I looked away because I also knew with a certainty if I laughed, she'd be on me like a lioness on its prey. She was bristling with aggression.

"A chance acquaintance," I said. "Tomas Severn," I added, remembering Tomas' last name just in time.

Logan-Evander looked up and beyond me. His eyes found Tomas, who was not looking over at us, and I saw the predatory way that Logan-Evander sized him up. Whatever else was going on, Logan-Evander was not impressed with poor Tomas.

"I think it's fair to say that Tomas is the one who benefits from the acquaintance," he murmured. "As do I."

I felt my cheeks warm. He was so charming, but it was offset by the danger that danced around him like a party guest.

"I don't know that it's safe for you to be here," I said.

Logan-Evander laughed, his big, loud rich laugh. While it was the same laugh I'd heard from Logan, Evander was more relaxed. More secure. He wasn't afraid of anything, or anyone.

There was a pause in the people around me, as they all looked over to see what was amusing him. He paid the heightened scrutiny no mind, instead leaning forward to whisper, "It's rarely safe for me, no matter where I find myself."

"Then why are you here?" I asked, feeling desperate. I knew who Logan was now. He'd be able to trace his past, find out what happened to him. But he didn't seem to have even the slightest worry about his situation.

"Because, my dear lady, business calls me to many places. I appreciate, however, your assessment of my safety." His eyes sharpened. "Is there some message you wish to deliver, a warning, perhaps?"

I nodded. I could do this, at least. "Yes. Those around you, the men, the women—they are not your friends. Not even your allies. They wish you ill."

"You can tell that how?" Logan-Evander ask, his gaze sharpening even more. He took a step closer to me.

"It's my talent," I said. "I see… intentions."

"That is a most useful talent to have. Would you like to have dinner with me?"

"Um…" I stopped. Tomas had spotted me, and was making his way over, his face alight with speculation and greed. How had I ever thought him attractive?

"Will you excuse me?" I looked up at Logan-Evander, and then at Tomas, and I did the only thing I knew to do.

I fled.

The moment I blended into the crowd, I closed my eyes. "Take me back," I said. "Right now."

When I opened my eyes, I was sitting on the back porch. The burner had burned down all the herbs, although the tea light was still trying to keep a feeble flame going. The sun had moved higher in the sky. It was late afternoon.

"Oh, hell!" I looked at my phone. Logan would be here soon. I'd been in my vision most of the afternoon. I could feel his triumph. He had some news.

And now, so did I.

I threw together homemade pizzas, and by the time Logan rang the doorbell, they were just about ready to come out of the oven.

When I answered the door, his face was alight in a way I hadn't seen before. "Wynter! I found something!"

"So did I," I said.

His eyes widened. "What? You did? What?"

"Come in, and let me tell you."

He came into the house, and I walked out onto the back porch. It was just before dusk, when the last light of the sun was moving downward in the sky.

"I know your name," I said.

"What?" Logan breathed behind me.

I nodded. "I've been spending time in the party, moving around the ballroom. I finally made it to the man I'd been wanting to see since the first time I fell into that party. The man who had his back to me every time I went in."

"Who was it?" Logan asked slowly.

I turned to face him. "It was you. Younger, with a different look. More polished. And your name was—is—Evander Thane."

"The name on the account is a subsidiary of Thane, Incorporated."

"Whatever you did as Evander, you were very well off, and very successful."

"It looks that way, from what I can tell about the company," Logan said.

"Everyone at that party hated you, in one way or another. They wanted something from you, or had to ask something, or owed you something, or envied you something. You didn't have one friend there."

Logan sat down. "Are you sure?"

I nodded. "I talked with you. You were very smooth, very urbane. I was so surprised to see that it was you that I told you danger was all around you, and you laughed and said, I know."

"So I knew I was surrounded by enemies."

"I don't know that for sure," I said, "But I would bet you did."

He stared off in the distance for what seemed a long time. Then he said, "Did you look up Evander Thane?"

"No. I wanted to wait until you got here. Besides, I overstayed in my vision, and I had to make dinner."

"Dinner could have waited," Logan said.

I sat down next to him, bringing my laptop from the side table between the chairs. "Let's see now."

I did an image search for Evander Thane, and the entire page filled with a variety of images. Evander in every sort of hot shot, playboy situation. He looked at ease in every picture. But his eyes, as I'd noticed at the party when I finally saw his face, were watchful.

It was definitely Logan.

He stared at the pictures, one after the other. "What happened to me?" he asked.

I shrugged. "I don't know. But I know where you can find out."

"Where?"

"529 Van der Veere Way, in Old Forge."

"Old Forge. Where is that?"

"Again, I didn't look, Logan. I wanted to wait until you were here. It's been a long time coming, this information. And look," I pointed at my laptop. "Someone filed a missing person's report on you."

"What?"

I opened the link. It was a detective, in New York city, asking for any information about Evander Thane. There was an email and a phone number at the bottom of the post.

He nodded, and opened a new window on the laptop to search. "Old Forge. It's in New York, too," he said. "A tiny place in upstate New York."

"Then you have to go there. Meet with the detective, and go to Old Forge."

"I do," Logan said slowly.

A realization hit me. "Logan, I did it."

"What?"

"I fulfilled your request. I did it. I made it through the test."

He stared at me for a moment, then he smiled. "You did! I was so wrapped up in my own stuff, I didn't even think about that. So that's it, right? You're the Oracle?"

I nodded. Now it was mine, to keep or to relinquish. No one, not some crazy lady and her bull, or some slick movie villain, could take it away. Although I had a feeling the blond man wouldn't be seen again for a long, long time.

It was mine.

After all this time of wanting to get rid of the responsibility of being the Oracle, I found I was reluctant to take the next steps. Goldie had been clear on what I needed to do, two days ago. Believing me ready to relinquish the Oracle, and him, he hadn't spoken to me since. I knew his feelings were hurt. I understood.

But now—I didn't think I wanted to let it go.

Then you must speak your desire aloud, I heard Goldie say quietly. *Step out into the yard, away from Logan, away from everyone else, and say, I accept.*

"That's it?" I asked.

That's it, Goldie replied.

"I'll be right back." Without waiting for a reply, I opened the screen door and went out into the back yard. The sun was nearly gone, the sky washed with deep pink and purple. I walked to the middle of the yard, and looked up. "I accept," I said.

The sky exploded in a shower of golden stars. I saw, out of the corner of my eye, Florry standing, her arms crossed, a cigarette in her hand and a smile on her face. I could make out shadowy figures behind her. Figures of women.

The Oracles.

They were all here.

For me.

The golden light moved around me, swirling faster and faster. But I didn't move, although my hair whipped around me.

I wondered how in the heck I was going to explain this to my neighbors. Although they hadn't seemed to notice anything else that had been going on lately, so maybe there would be nothing that needed explanation.

And if there was, I realized, I could manage it.

Because I was the Oracle of Theama. I had been chosen, and I accepted the gift. This was who I was, and who I would be.

By my choice.

The golden light around me faded, as did all of the shadowy figures around Florry.

You made the right choice, Goldie said. He actually sounded happy.

"Yes, you did," Florry agreed. "Wasn't sure you'd do it."

"Neither was I," I said.

"Now things will really get interesting," Florry said.

"What, this was low key?"

"Kind of," Florry shrugged. "Go in and help your consultant. And get used to how he is now. Lots of 'em are gonna be that way. Stunned, unable to believe it. They need your help after you give them the answers they're looking for. You can't just boot them out, much as you might want to."

"Makes sense," I said. Not only was Logan my consultant, he'd become a friend. And he'd been there for me as I stumbled through learning how to try and be the Oracle.

This was the least I could do for him.

I walked back onto the porch. "So. You want to talk about this? What your next steps should be?" I was smiling as I sat down.

CHAPTER SIXTEEN

Two Weeks Later

I sat on the edge of the bed, my hands threading and re-threading themselves together. I was waiting for my kids to finish getting ready. We were in Phoenix.

A few days after I'd accepted the Oracle, I'd gotten an email.

Dear Wynter,

Thank you for your email. I'm sure you can understand that I wasn't able to reply immediately. Learning that Derek lied to me, that he had an entirely different life—I have been struggling since I was told about you, and your children.

I know that you probably understand, although I don't presume to know you.

But your email was very kind, and I kept coming back to it. Whatever else there may be between you and I, our children share a parent, and I would like them to meet, to know that they have more family. No matter how the ties came about.

If you and your children are willing, I would like to invite all of you to come to Phoenix for a weekend, to meet each other, and to see where things might lead.

Please let me know your thoughts on this.

Sincerely,

Natalie Chastain

I'd sent the email to all three of the kids, asking for their feedback. Rachel had said we shouldn't go.

"Why?" I asked.

"Because this is the icy polite email of a woman who is deeply pissed, and since Dad's not here for her to take a bite out of, she's going to bite you."

"She can try," I said, secure in the knowledge that nothing my late husband's second wife could say to me would hurt. If she went after my children, there would be trouble. But other than that? I was feeling calm. I mean, if she wanted to get nasty, I was the first wife, the legal wife.

I didn't think we'd get to that point. But Rachel was right. I read the underlying anger as well. However, we'd discussed it as a family, and the kids decided that if I was all right with it, they would go along with my decision.

"She insults you once, though, and we're out of there," Kris said now. "Rachel," he turned to look toward the bathroom of our hotel room. "Come on. You're going to make us late!"

"Oh, she might insult me more than once. She's hurt. It happens," I said.

"You're taking this really well, Mom," Theo said.

"None of this will bring your dad back. And whatever else he was, he was a good father to you kids. He loved you."

"He loved you, too," Kris said quickly.

"I think he did. But he stepped on that love, and there's no changing that. Listen," I raised my voice a little as Rachel joined us. "I love that the three of you are ready to take up arms on my behalf but I don't want you to. Well, not right now. If I decide I need to be offended and hair flip out of there, I'll let you know.

Otherwise, try and ignore anything that might sound catty, or snide, or whatever."

"It won't be easy," Rachel said.

"Remember why we're here. It's not for me, or Natalie. It's for you three, and Nathan and Sophie."

That softened them, as I knew it would. I figured that there would be bumps in this new relationship, but I knew that it would happen, and my kids would be the better for it. So would their brother and sister.

I didn't have a clear picture of what might happen between me and Natalie. I'd stewed over this for a bit before coming to the conclusion that I couldn't tell because it didn't matter.

It was the kids who mattered.

And after that, it was easy.

We'd flown in yesterday, had dinner, and gone to bed early. Now we were ready to go over and have lunch.

"I'll drive," Theo said.

Everyone was quiet in the car, lost in their own thoughts. I checked my phone. Logan had left for Old Forge four days ago, to scout out the house on Van der Veere Way, and see what he could find out about the owners. When he asked me, I told him that going in carefully was his best course of action.

I was glad to see that he was listening.

But I hadn't heard from him since yesterday morning. The lack of communication was starting to make me feel on edge. We would need to work on what it meant to keep someone posted on what was going on. He was decidedly bad at it.

Two days ago, I'd gotten a call from someone who identified themselves as the supernatural police, for lack of a better word. They had been made aware, how they didn't say, that I was the new Oracle of Theama. I emailed them back, agreeing to set up an appointment with them next week. I also had a feeling that while I wasn't done helping Logan, I had another consultant coming toward me. Or maybe I just wanted one, now that I'd made my decision. Either way, all that was next week, after my kids were long gone, and back in their lives.

Right now was for them. I moved all my Oracle concerns to the side, and let my kids have all my attention.

Theo turned the car down a street that ended in a cul-de-sac. "That's it," he said, peering out and pointing at a house that sat right in the middle of the cul-de-sac.

He pulled into the driveway and before he'd even turned off the car, the door of the house opened, showing two little kids in the doorway. I could just see the taller woman behind them.

I'd faced down a lot in the last month. This was cake, comparatively. "Come on," I said to the kids. "Let's go."

I opened the door and put a smile on my face.

The End

I hope you enjoyed Hexes & Hot Flashes. Wynter moves further into the life of the Oracle in book two, Magic & Menopause.

http:// smarturl.it/MagicNMenopause

Five weeks ago, I might have killed a man. Five days ago, I met my husband's other wife. Five minutes ago, a dead body washed ashore. Just another day in the life of an Oracle, right?

I thought taking care of the hex that wanted to kill me was all I had to worry about, but then Farrah Lockwood arrives on my porch with a new mystery. She thinks she's come to me for advice but the fact she found me at all means there are bigger things afoot... much bigger. What seems like a simple matter of whodunit quickly becomes deeper and I find myself strapped in and holding tight on a roller coaster ride into an ancient Egyptian curse, a pair of secret societies about to go to war with each other, and a rather alarming revelation that my new friend Logan is tied up in this as well.

I had just settled into the idea of being a widow when all this Oracle business landed on my arm. Now, the threats that follow Farrah have arrived on my doorstep and there's more at stake than any of us know. Did I forget to mention my doctor has confirmed I'm in menopause and all of this is getting on my last nerve?

Once upon a time, I imagined forty-five would find me dealing with an empty nest and planning for retirement. I never thought I'd be so single, so sweaty, and fighting to stay alive.

Age may be just a number, but I swear all this drama is making me one grouchy Oracle.

One Click Magic & Menopause now.

Stay up to date on my newest releases by signing up for my Newsletter... www.lisamanifold.com/news

Love the strong older women with more than a little magic? Then you'll love The Deadwood Sisters. They may look like twenty-somethings, but in reality, they are more like one-hundred and twenty. They protect Deadwood. No exceptions.

Are you a mystery fan who likes your suspense with a touch of romance? Then check out The Mostly Open Paranormal Investigative Agency series, complete with a witch, a vampire, and a maddening demon and where being cursed is a family affair.

Don't miss a release, a sneak peak, cover reveals, and more. Sign up for my Newsletter!

Thank you so much for being a reader, and spreading the word, which includes telling a friend. Reviews are how readers find new books and new authors to love. Please leave a review on your favorite book site.

XO,

Lisa

Keep reading for an excerpt from Magic & Menopause.

Chapter One

I stared at the doctor, the disorientation hitting hard. "You want to do what?" Usually she made my yearly physical seem like visiting with a friend, but this time, not.

I didn't know what was wrong with me this afternoon, but I'd been asking people to repeat themselves far too often. My daughter, my best friend Shelly, even the the receptionist when she'd asked for my payment earlier, and now my doctor, Dr. Chloe Amberson. Everyone seemed to speak a shorthand I could not comprehend.

"Wynter, we can find out if this is menopause pretty easily." She gave me her you-know-you've-got-to-do-this smile. "We'll take some blood, and that's all. Voila!" She nodded like I'd already agreed. "Then we'll know, one way or another." Her voice is bouncy and bright to disguise the grenade she's setting off in my life.

"It can't be menopause." My forehead crinkled. "It just… can't." I had powers, magic supposedly. Not menopause. Magic. Couldn't I stop this? Wasn't there some kind of anti-aging potion?

"Why? Because the hot flashes are symptomatic of say, gout?" Dr. Amberson's words hit me all wrong, wrong, wrong. "Are you cold?"

"I'm sorry, what?" Her sudden change of subject threw me off.

"Right now. Are you cold?"

"No, which is weird. Normally, I'm freezing in here." I indicated the sweater sitting on the chair opposite me under my purse. Then I looked up at Dr. Amberson. My mouth was partially open, probably shock.

"You're just proving my point."

"I cannot be in menopause." I stared off at the wall. This would be one more damn thing in this month of damn things.

"You're ahead of the game if you find out when all you're dealing with is hot flashes."

"What else is there?" I asked. Like the hot flashes weren't bad enough? There was more? "I'm too young for this. I'm not even fifty."

"We all go through it." She patted my shoulder. "I survived. You'll survive."

The fluorescent light in the room crackled, which made me jump. All of a sudden, I could smell the alcohol in the sanitizer she'd used when she'd first come in, sharp and biting. I could smell the air conditioning in the room, even if I didn't feel it. But I knew I wasn't pregnant, which was the last time I noticed things crazy like this.

Oh, God. Menopause.

"Let's take some blood, and then we'll know." She was all business.

"What else can I expect?"

"Hmm?" Dr. Amberson held up the needle she had in her hand.

"What else can I expect from menopause?" I repeated myself, wanting to make sure I'd get the information I needed. "Other symptoms, that kind of thing."

"Oh," she turned around, needle still in hand. "You tend to sweat more at night. Weight gain, and your metabolism shifts. Insomnia. Don't worry about it right now, Wynter." Her smile dropped away. "Wait. You haven't been looking up your symptoms, have you?" Her eyes got fierce.

Whoa.

"No. I haven't looked up a thing." I wasn't lying. Like I'd admit it if I was. She was downright scary at the moment.

With everything that had been going on—the death of my husband in a helicopter crash, learning he had another life, another wife, and even other kids, for one thing. Then helping my own kids deal with these facts about their father. That was still tough.

Add to that finding out that I was a magical being called the Oracle of Theama, with Logan (a consultant seeking my help as the Oracle) and Florry (the former Oracle)—my recent hot flashes had just been one more annoying thing I needed to deal with. I didn't have the time to look into them. My sweating just wasn't high on my list of concerns.

With what I'd been through the last month, I felt like sweating more than normal was appropriate. I'd already escaped being killed by random scary men.

"Good. When you start to search via search engines or medical websites for reasons for your symptoms, you either have cancer, or you're going to die soon," Dr. Amberson said, bringing me back to our conversation.

Despite my stress over the idea that I might be in menopause, I laughed. "I used to see that when I'd look up things for the kids."

She rolled her eyes. "The people who write most of the medical symptoms should lose internet privileges. I get more people in here scared to death based on something they read."

"So you're saying I should be grateful it's just menopause?"

"Not at all. Menopause is just another step in the female reproductive system, one that requires us to manage it and live with it. It's not fun."

"Par for the course," I said.

"Exactly. So my job is to find out if that is what this really is and help you ease the symptoms. I don't believe in just having to live with it."

Hearing her, with her matter-of-fact approach, made me feel better.

"Which arm?" Dr. Amberson waved the needle at me.

I stuck out my right arm, pushing up my sleeve.

There was a silence.

"When did you get a tattoo?" Dr. Amberson asked.

One click Magic & Menopause now.

ACKNOWLEDGMENTS

This has been such a fun book. I first read work in this genre, Paranormal Women's Fiction, at the beginning of 2020. I was instantly hooked. I had no plans to branch out into any other genres, but once I made it through the #Fab13 s books, I knew I wanted to write it. It's just so great. I love the older heroine, dealing with different aspects of life than I usually write about.

And the readers- wow! I've been in reader groups, following along as the readers discovered this genre, and they are amazing.

I hope you enjoyed it as much I enjoyed writing it. Book Two, Magic & Menopause, will be out later in the year.

January 2021

Lisa Manifold

ABOUT THE AUTHOR

Lisa Manifold is a *USA Today* Bestselling Author of fantasy, paranormal, and romance stories. She moved to Rocky Mountains of Colorado as an adult and has no plans of living anywhere else. She is a consummate reader, often running late because "Just one more page!"

Lisa is the author of many flavors of paranormal series. She writes what she does in the hopes that one day, the Goblin King will come and take her away. (Should he do so, she's staying, by the way.)

She lives in the mountains of Colorado with her children, and rescued #reddogs and one murder cat.

Stay in touch:
Sign up for her Newsletter and never miss a thing!
Website: www.lisamanifold.com
Or one of the links below.
And hey - if you've read Maximum Security Magic, you can download the free prequel, Undercover Vamp.
Xoxo
Lisa

(books written with a collective of authors)

A Midnight Coven Anthology

Tempted by Fae

Cursed Coven Series

Wicked Love

Vampire Mates Series

Immortal Darkness

Vampire Brides Series

Forever Blood

The Dragon Thief

Dragon Lost

Dragon Found

The Realm Series

Heart of the Goblin King

To Wed the Goblin King

Realms of the Goblin King

Rise of the Dragon King

The Companion Tales, Volume I

The Companion Tales, Volume II

The Aumahnee Prophecy

with Corinne O'Flynn

Made in the USA
Las Vegas, NV
20 August 2021